To remember what you've W9-CYH-757

initials in a square!

47

1538

LAWYER
for the
DOG

Center Point
Large Print

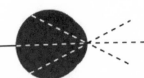

**This Large Print Book carries the
Seal of Approval of N.A.V.H.**

LAWYER
for the
DOG

Lee Robinson

CENTER POINT LARGE PRINT
THORNDIKE, MAINE

This Center Point Large Print edition
is published in the year 2016 by arrangement with
St. Martin's Press.

Original text on pages 108–109 is from
The Boston Globe, "Lawyer for the Dog,"
by Drake Bennett, September 9, 2007.

Original text on pages 270–271 is from
Travels with Charley, by John Steinbeck © 1962.

The text of this Large Print edition is unabridged.
In other aspects, this book may vary from the original edition.
Printed in the United States of America on permanent paper.
Set in 16-point Times New Roman type.

ISBN: 978-1-62899-868-9

Library of Congress Cataloging-in-Publication Data

Names: Robinson, Lee, 1948- author.
Title: Lawyer for the dog / Lee Robinson.
Description: Center Point Large Print edition. | Thorndike, Maine :
Center Point Large Print, 2016. | ©2015
Identifiers: LCCN 2015042521 | ISBN 9781628998689
    (hardcover : alk. paper)
Subjects: LCSH: Women lawyers—Fiction. | Divorced women—Fiction.
| Dog owners—Fiction. | Large type books.
Classification: LCC PS3618.O329 L39 2016 | DDC 813/.6—dc23
LC record available at http://lccn.loc.gov/2015042521

for Jerry, always

Acknowledgments

I am deeply grateful to Ann Stirling, Michael O'Connell, Jane Dowling Fender, Bonnie Lyons, Susan Schmidt, Sarah Steinhardt, Charles Merrill, Salley McInerney, Abraham Verghese, Alan Shapiro, Steven Kellman, and Wendy Barker; and to all the folks at Gemini Ink for their encouragement and help with this book; to Mary Evans, agent extraordinaire, for her faith in it; and to everyone at Thomas Dunne Books for nurturing it.

The late Maxine Kumin, my friend and mentor, read an early draft and made many valuable suggestions. I miss her keen mind and her literary mothering.

Thanks to my family folks, near and far, for your support and your stories, especially to my children, Luke and Sally, who endured my lawyering days.

I am indebted most of all to my husband, Jerry Winakur, for his love and patience through many drafts, and for his always insightful comments.

LAWYER
for the
DOG

The Brief of My Life

I've defended murderers, rapists, burglars, and drug dealers. In my public defender days I represented a woman who threw her baby off a bridge and an eighty-year-old granny who whacked her husband with a frying pan when he complained about her cooking. You name a heinous crime or a major human transgression, and I've defended it. Or imagine the worst marriage in the history of the world, and I've represented the worst half of it.

And now what?

"I need a big favor," said Joe Baynard, judge of the Charleston County Family Court, when he called this morning. He's forty-nine, just a couple of days younger than I am, but otherwise we are totally unalike, which is why, come to think of it, I fell in love with him, and also probably why he is now my ex.

"No more pro bonos," I protested. I already had six or seven court-appointed cases on my plate, cases for which I would be paid next-to-nothing for God knows how many hours of work.

"Let me tell you about the case," Joe said. We were on the telephone, but I knew from the tone of his voice that he was picking his fingernails and heard him slide open his desk drawer to deposit a sliver. He always picks his fingernails when he's agitated.

"One of these days Betty's going to find your stash," I said. Betty is his secretary.

"What?"

"All those fingernails."

"I empty the drawer once a week now."

"I guess even the most hardened criminals can be reformed," I said.

I heard him close the drawer. "I really need your help, Sally."

I hated it when he got like this. It brought back all the guilt. Why couldn't I just despise him, like any normal ex-wife?

"But aside from doing me a favor, it's a really fascinating case," he continued.

"Last time I took one of your 'fascinating' cases, I had to borrow money to keep my practice going." I'll never forget that one: he'd appointed me to represent a nine-year-old in a custody battle that went on for two years—with motion hearing after motion hearing, a six-week trial—at the end of which the dad, who'd been ordered to pay my fees, disappeared.

"There's plenty of money in this one," Joe said. "I'm going to order some interim fees to whoever represents the dog."

"The dog?"

"He's a schnauzer."

"Are you kidding?"

I heard him shuffle some papers. "Yeah, that's right. A *miniature* schnauzer."

"Since when does a dog need a lawyer?"

"This dog needs one. I'll have Betty copy the file for you, so you can get up to speed."

"Joe," I tried to sound firm, "I don't represent dogs. I don't even know why—"

"If I'm not mistaken, you've represented plenty of dogs in your time. Plenty."

"Ha, ha."

"And this particular dog is charming."

"I don't like dogs."

"I have a picture right here . . . very cute dog. So, you'll do it?"

"Explain why a schnauzer needs a lawyer."

"Because he's tying up the case, and the case is tying up my court. I'm surprised you haven't heard about it," said Joe. His voice broke. "I feel like . . . like I'm losing control."

"Are you okay?"

"Can we have lunch today?" he pleaded.

"I don't think Susan would like that very much." Susan is Joe's wife.

"We can eat in my chambers."

"I don't think that's a good idea."

"We've been divorced for eighteen years," he said. "You think anyone cares if we have lunch together to talk about a case?"

"Susan might."

"Believe me, Susan doesn't care." Was that bitterness in his voice, or was I imagining it? "I'll ask Betty to order some takeout. You still a vegetarian?"

"Yes, but not vegan anymore."

"Just tell me what you eat."

"Vegetables. Cheese. Beans. No meat."

"What about one of those Greek salads from Dino's?"

"Fine. Dressing on the side."

"It's great that you're still a vegetarian," he said.

"You always thought it was an affectation."

"But it's good for the dog . . ."

"What?"

"I mean for your relationship with the dog."

"I don't have relationships with dogs," I said.

"I could argue with that."

"Anyway, what difference would it make to the dog . . . my being a vegetarian?"

"It shows respect for animals," Joe said. "I have my lunch break at one thirty. You'll be here?"

"I'm preparing for a trial."

"*Please,* Sally."

He hadn't said "please" that way since the day I left him.

My favorite law school professor used to say that the most important thing about a legal brief is that it be what it claims to be: *brief.* State the facts concisely, he'd say, without losing anything essential. Judges don't have time for irrelevant information, no matter how interesting. Make your arguments in plain language. Nobody wants to wade through a swamp of "therefores" and "howevers" and twisted syntax.

"If you had only twenty-five words to state the facts of your life," this professor used to say, "what would you write?"

> Sarah Bright Baynard, b. Columbia, South Carolina
>
> B.A. University of South Carolina, magna cum laude
>
> J.D. University of South Carolina Law School
>
> Married Joseph Henry Baynard, divorced after five years

True enough so far, but I've left out that afternoon when Joseph Henry Baynard took Sarah Bright, aka Sally, to his basement apartment near the law school, luring her with a plea for help with Constitutional Law, but mixing Constitutional Law with a little vodka and tonic and some Beatles on the boom box. Somehow Joe and Sally found themselves dancing and laughing, then falling exhausted onto Joe's sofa (that threadbare thing he'd covered with a batik bedspread) and laughing some more, then kissing, both surprised at how good the kissing was.

In the Brief of My Life, doesn't that afternoon matter as much as my birthplace, my degrees? My career?

Assistant Public Defender
Associate, Baynard, Baker, and Gibson, Charleston, South Carolina
Chief Public Defender, Charleston County
Solo practice, Sarah B. Baynard, LLC

And in the Brief of My Life, what about that morning in the ladies' room of Baynard, Baker, and Gibson—Joe's family firm, the venerable firm of his father and his grandfather—my head bent to my knees, the pain I'd been ignoring all morning grinding deeper in my pelvis? I hadn't even been sure I was pregnant. I was doing my best that morning not to think about it, but this miscarriage was undeniable, and with it the other things I didn't want to think about: my misery at the firm ("You never even tried to fit in," said Joe) and my failure as a wife ("You never really wanted this marriage, did you?").

What really matters in the Brief of Life, as I'm just now beginning to understand, is what you won't read about yourself in the alumni news or your local newspaper—your loves, your joys, your losses, your grief. That grief that almost pulled you under, the quiet daily struggle just to stay sane.

If I died today, in this my forty-ninth year, you'd see my obituary in tomorrow's *Post and Courier*. If you stopped to read it, perhaps you'd be impressed by a life so full of accomplishments. You'd have no clue, reading that Final Brief, what a mess I've made of it.

The file for *Hart v. Hart* is really a collection of files, enough to fill a cardboard box.

"Betty's working on copies for you, but it may take a while," Joe says. He's already started on his chicken sandwich.

"I haven't agreed to take the case." Nevertheless I reach for the file labeled *Pleadings*.

"Eat your lunch while I give you a summary," he says. The salad is drowning in dressing, but I'm hungry. "Mrs. Hart filed for divorce at the end of July—"

"Jesus. All that paper already?" I motion toward the files.

"I told you, the case is out of control."

"Who represents the wife?"

"Henry Swinton."

"That weasel."

"It would be improper for me to comment," Joe says, winking.

"And the husband? Who's the lucky lawyer?"

"Michelle Marvel."

"She of the marvelous short skirts and low-cut blouses?"

"I never noticed."

"Right."

"She's smart as hell," he says.

"Smart enough to use that short-skirt-and-sweet-smile routine to throw you off guard until she opens her mouth and venom comes out."

"That's going a bit far," says Joe.

"I said it, not you."

"But so far," I talk through a mouthful of salad, "you haven't exactly won me over."

"I never *could* win you over." There's a catch in his voice that makes me nervous.

"Don't start."

"Anyway," he continues, "Mrs. Hart alleges that her husband has committed adultery. He counter-claims habitual drunkenness. They've been married for almost forty years."

"So, they must be at least in their sixties?"

Joe nods. "She's living in their beach house, Sullivan's Island. He's in the house downtown . . . East Battery."

"What about assets?"

"They won't be starving anytime soon. The real estate alone is worth a fortune."

"I don't get it. This seems like your standard rich people's divorce. Some boozing, some playing around, assets to be valued and divided—probably close to fifty-fifty—maybe some alimony, but no minor children, no custody battle. So what do you need *me* for?"

"It's the dog, Sally. They're fighting over the dog."

"The dog is just personal property. No different, in the eyes of the law, than a car or a chair or a pair of candlesticks, right?"

"This dog is different," he says. "He's tying up the case. He has the potential to tie up my whole docket. This dog needs a lawyer."

"I fail to see how throwing another lawyer into the mix is going to—"

"Actually, what I have in mind is more like a guardian ad litem. Somebody to protect the interests of the dog, do an investigation, make a recommendation to the court, just like in a custody case. And somebody who just might shine the light of reason on the situation. I'm going to appoint you on my own motion, unless they object," Joe says.

"This is ridiculous!"

"There's a hearing Monday, ten a.m. You might want to do a little research beforehand. If this were *your* dog, wouldn't you want the best for him?"

"I've never even . . . I mean, it's been a long time since I've had a dog."

"I remember. One of your cardinal rules for an uncomplicated life: no dogs. No houseplants. And no more husbands." He smiles. Everything dear about him is in that smile. I stand up to go. I want to get away from the flush rising up my neck to my cheeks.

"But you do have a lot of common sense and a low tolerance for bullshit, which is why I need you on this case," Joe continues. "By the way, how's your mother?"

"She has Alzheimer's." My mother has lived with me since the diagnosis two years ago.

"I'm sorry to hear that. Give her my regards, would you?"

"And you give my best to Susan."

"I would, except we're separated."

"Oh, Joe, I'm sorry. When?"

"A couple of weeks ago. It's a long story. I won't bore you with it." I know him well enough to know he really means *Please listen,* but I can't stay. After all this time I still feel our breakup like a sharp pain, an old wound that flares up just when I think I'm fully healed. "Thanks for doing this, Sally."

"You take care of yourself," I say. We shake hands, and I'm almost out of the door when he says, "His name is Sherman."

"What?"

"The dog's name is Sherman."

Lost Something

I don't have children, but I'm not childless. My mother is my child.

Every morning I wake her and make her breakfast. I coax her into finishing her scrambled eggs, bribe her with the promise of a Milky Way if she'll take her pills. On weekdays I settle her in front of the TV with the morning paper, which she pretends to read until Delores, the sitter, comes at eight. Delores is a cross between a saint and a drill sergeant, with infinite patience and a no-nonsense toughness that my mother respects. Without Delores, we'd be lost.

Even so, I call home two or three times a day to make sure things are going okay. After work I fix my mother's dinner, rotating her old favorites: spaghetti and meatballs, baked chicken, pork chops. I don't eat these things anymore, but I like having someone to cook for. Most of the time she has a good appetite, but every now and then she refuses to eat. "Don't wait," she says, pushing her plate toward me. She means, "Don't waste."

"I'm a vegetarian, remember?"

But of course she doesn't remember. After dinner I help her into the shower, help her lower herself onto the plastic chair she uses so she won't fall. I wait close by until she finishes, retrieve the soap when she drops it, make sure she washes thoroughly. After the shower I sit her on the end of her bed and help her work her arms through the sleeves of her nightgown, tuck her in, and then I read to her, her old favorites— *Travels with Charley*, *The Wind in the Willows*— until she falls asleep.

On weekends Delores is off, and though I sometimes use another sitter, my mother doesn't like her, so I spend most of my time at home. If I have work to do—which is almost always—I put Mom in front of the TV or let her listen to Frank Sinatra with earphones.

Sometimes we sit on my little balcony over-looking Charleston harbor. The balcony is a blessing, which makes up for living in this otherwise charmless high-rise. I give my mother the binoculars, and she'll watch the sailboats and the container ships go by while I work at my laptop.

She has good days and bad days. On her good days she can be talkative, even comprehensible, but this is a bad day and she is mostly silent, every now and then uttering a single word— "bird" or "flag" or "boat,"—and then I'll look out at the water, too, grateful that her mind can still connect to an object and name it. Occasionally she'll say something that seems to come from nowhere, like "Isn't it a mystery?" or "Forgot my umbrella" and rather than confuse her with a query, I simply nod and say yes.

Most Sunday mornings I drive her to Grace Episcopal Church for the eleven o'clock service. We sit near the back in case she wants to leave before the service is over, but most of the time she can make it through the whole hour. She has trouble remembering the prayers and she can't follow the words in the hymn book anymore, but sometimes I hear her humming along. I can't tell how much of the sermon she understands but at least she seems soothed by the sound of the minister's voice, or perhaps she's pleased just to have her daughter sitting next to her in church.

Her doctor has warned me that these relatively peaceful days won't last forever, that her "spells"— outbursts of agitation or anxiety in which she cries for no reason and paces back and forth in front of the TV, or wakes at night screaming—will come more often, and that she may stop eating.

"What will you do then?" Ellen asks. Ellen Sadler is my best friend, a prosecutor with a heart, as close to a well-balanced person as I've ever known.

"I guess I'll have to buy those liquid supplements. I think she'd like the chocolate."

"No," says Ellen, "I mean, when you can't keep her at home."

"I can't think that far ahead." This isn't true, because of course I've thought about it. The truth is that I hope my mother will die before I have to make that decision. I can hardly admit this to myself, much less to my friend. And it isn't just that I want my mother to die for *her* sake—how many times did I hear her say she wouldn't want to live if her mind were gone?—but I want her to die for *my* sake, because I'm not at all sure I'm capable of mothering my mother much longer, and I promised her I'd never put her in a nursing home.

"Well, you know I'm here for you," says Ellen. And she is, of course, but even Ellen can't put herself in my place, can't imagine what it's like. Nobody can, unless they're living it. "Are you coming to the book club meeting?" she asks.

"I haven't read the book."

"Come anyway. You haven't been in months," she says. "Want me to pick you up?"

"I'd have to arrange for the night sitter . . ."

"You can't just hole up every night with your mother," Ellen says. "She wouldn't want that for you."

Ellen is right, of course. But then almost nothing about my life is what my mother wanted for me.

My mother wanted me to get just enough education to carry on an intelligent conversation, but not so much, God forbid, that anyone would ever mistake me for an "intellectual." She wanted me to be able to earn a living, but only on a temporary basis while I supported a husband through law or medical school, or in case of dire emergency, such as sudden widowhood. "You'd make a wonderful administrative secretary," she'd say, "or a teacher." She'd gone back to teaching after my father died. But—though she never actually said this, I knew what she thought—it would be a bad idea for me to think about a *career.* "Those women can be so . . . oh, you know . . . men don't like them."

My mother wanted me to have children—two or three, more than that would be tacky—and do volunteer work with the Junior League and church committees and learn to play a civilized sport that would keep me from getting fat. Tennis or golf, maybe, with stylish outfits.

She wanted me to have a nice house, kept spotless by a maid who'd come no less than twice a week, and a big yard full of azaleas and camellias, tended to by a black man who knew to knock on the back door if he needed something but did not expect to be invited inside.

What she wanted for me was what she'd always wanted for herself.

The night before the first hearing in *Hart v. Hart,* Mom and I sit on the balcony at sundown. I do some research on my laptop while she watches a Navy cruiser head out toward the ocean. When it's time to go inside she says, "Lost something." She's always losing things—the TV remote, her purse, her toothbrush—but this time she points to the photograph that has slipped out of the file and fallen to the floor.

I reach down to get it. "Want to see my newest client?" I ask her. "His name is Sherman."

She studies the photo, runs her index finger over the dog's face: lively dark eyes, long whiskers, pert black nose. Then she hands the photo to me. "I'm so sorry . . ." she says, her voice, as always these days, a little shaky.

"What, Mom? What are you sorry about?"

"Our dog . . ."

"We don't have a dog."

"Brownie."

"That was a long time ago. Don't worry about it. You thought you were doing the best thing for him."

"He might . . . He might come back."

"No, Mom. He won't come back. You gave him away, remember?"

But of course she doesn't remember.

Love Gone Bad

In a country where half of all marriages fail, we're still pretending divorce doesn't exist, and Courtroom 4 of the Charleston County Family Court reflects that. It's a cramped room—nothing like the grand space of the "big court," the criminal court, which has a different set of judges and a great deal more prestige. Family court is a world unto itself, a court with an inferiority complex, and though the county has just spent millions on renovations, no amount of money can change that. It's a place of sadness and secrets, booze and bruised faces, battered lives. There are no juries here, just the beleaguered judges who sit day after day listening to the latest installment of "Love Gone Bad."

My ex-husband Joe, who's been a judge for ten years now, says family court is where we hide our dirty laundry. In the criminal court, we air it out. During particularly gruesome murder cases the benches are packed with people. Here in family court, though the proceedings are technically open to the public, there's a tradition of secrecy and barely enough room in the courtrooms for the litigants and their lawyers.

It's strange: The most sensational and gruesome murders may shock us, frighten us, but they don't

27

shame us, because we think of the accused on trial downstairs as not at all like us. He's another kind of being, a "monster," a "maniac." He's evil. We tell ourselves we could never do what he's accused of. The sins that truly threaten us, that fill the transcripts of the family court, are the private betrayals, the quiet little violations that go on every day in our homes and families. If we haven't yet committed sins like these, we know we're capable of them.

I sit on one of the two benches behind Mrs. Hart and her lawyer, Henry Swinton. On the other side of the courtroom are Mr. Hart and Michelle Marvel. We rise when the court reporter comes in and expect the judge to follow, but the reporter's just retrieving a file from the last hearing, so we'll wait some more. Mrs. Hart and Henry Swinton ignore me, conferring with each other in whispers and mumbles. Michelle Marvel takes this opportunity to shake my hand. Her lips open to reveal her very white and remarkably straight teeth, teeth made even more startling by her thick red lipstick.

"This is my old friend Sally Baynard," Michelle says to her client, although we are not and have never been friends. "Sally, this is Rusty Hart." Mr. Hart doesn't look capable of committing adultery, though I try not to jump to conclusions. Every-thing about him has gone gray: his eyebrows, which need trimming, his sparse hair, even his eyes. The buttons of his gray jacket strain against the push of his belly.

"Baynard," he says to me, "Isn't that the judge's name?"

Michelle Marvel jumps in before I can answer. "We can talk about that later, Rusty." She pulls him back to his seat. Mrs. Hart and Henry Swinton are still whispering, their heads almost touching. They could be a couple, though I know Henry's at least a decade younger. They both have the same impeccable rich-Southern-White-Protestant taste in clothes and trim, well-maintained bodies.

At last the court reporter opens the door behind the bench. "All rise," she says. Joe follows close behind in his rumpled black robe. He once told me how much he hates the robe. What he really means is that he hates his job. He thought it would be a stepping-stone to a judgeship in the big court. It wasn't. His family connections won't be enough anymore, and he dreads the politicking and the necessary self-promotion.

"Please be seated," Joe says. He opens the file, nods to the court reporter. "Motion hearing in the case of Maryann S. Hart v. Russell B. Hart. Actually, two motions. Mrs. Hart requests a reconsideration of the court's temporary order insofar as it gives her possession of the residence on Sullivan's Island, and Mr. Hart moves for temporary custody of the dog, who . . . ah . . . which . . . who is now, ah, in Mrs. Hart's possession. The parties have both submitted affidavits in support of their positions."

Henry Swinton rises as quickly as pomposity will allow. "Your honor, it's my client's position that the motion for custody of the dog should be dismissed as a matter of law. A dog is not—"

Judge Baynard has anticipated this. "We'll hear Mrs. Hart's motion first, since it was filed first. Mr. Swinton, please tell me why it is necessary—pending a trial of this case—for your client to move out of the Sullivan's Island house into the home downtown. As I'm sure I don't need to remind you, the court is not inclined to modify temporary orders."

"Your honor, as you know, Mrs. Hart's decision to separate was not made without a great deal of—"

"Mr. Swinton, tell me what's changed here. A month ago your client said she preferred to stay in the beach house until trial."

"Yessir, that was our position, but Mrs. Hart has found it too painful"—at this point Swinton pats his client's shoulder as she dabs her eyes with a tissue—"to live in the house that was the scene of Mr. Hart's adulterous relationship."

Michelle Marvel rockets upward, her short skirt showing off her legs in all their glory. "My client absolutely denies any such conduct," she shouts, "and further, Mrs. Hart had already obtained the detective's report—which, by the way, certainly doesn't establish adultery—before the first hearing in this case, when she asked for temporary possession of the beach house."

"I'm not deaf, Ms. Marvel," Joe says, "and nobody in this room is deaf. Now," he nods toward Henry Swinton, "I'm waiting for you to tell me why your client can't make herself happy—not forever, mind you, but only until a trial in this case—in a nice house on the front beach in one of the best communities on the East Coast."

"Judge," Henry Swinton perseveres, "Mr. Hart's paramour lives next door to the Sullivan's Island home. Under the circumstances, Mrs. Hart feels—"

A protest rumbles up through Rusty Hart's throat and explodes into the air. "Paramour? That girl's not my *paramour*, for God's sake. She's just a friend. But while we're on the subject, why don't you ask my wife what she does when she disappears for hours at—"

Judge Baynard cuts him off, but kindly. "I'm afraid you'll have to let your lawyer do the talking, Mr. Hart. Mr. Swinton, anything else?"

"As your honor will see from my client's affidavit, she also feels that Mr. Hart isn't able to manage the housekeeping at the downtown house. Friends have reported that the place is a mess."

"Isn't there a maid?" asks Judge Baynard.

"I seem to recall that there are maids for both houses, isn't that right?"

"Yessir," replies Swinton, "but as your honor can imagine, the maid needs supervision, and this is especially necessary in the downtown home, which is three floors and, uh, approximately twelve thousand square feet. Mrs. Hart—"

At this point Michelle Marvel rises to speak, but before she can get the words out, Joe Baynard issues his ruling: "I don't see any change of circumstances or urgency here. Plaintiff's motion denied. Now, before we move on to the motion about the dog, let me explain why I've asked Sarah Baynard to be here. This is the . . ." He flips through several pages of the file in front of him. ". . . third or fourth motion involving the dog, if I'm not mistaken. I'm a dog lover myself, but family court judges have their work cut out for them just trying to take care of human beings, so, as I notified you all several days ago, I've asked Ms. Baynard to serve as guardian ad litem for Sherman, and to assist me in providing for his welfare. Do either of you lawyers have any objection?"

Henry Swinton rises. "Your honor, our objection is not to Ms. Baynard. We all know," and now he turns around to face me, his voice saccharine, "what an outstanding attorney she is, what a tremendous asset to the Charleston bar—"

"Succinctly, Mr. Swinton," says Judge Baynard.

Swinton clears his throat. "Our objection is not to Ms. Baynard, but to the notion that an animal is entitled to a guardian. We're not talking about custody here."

"You could have fooled me," says Judge Baynard.

Swinton continues: "While my client adores Sherman, she does not elevate him to the status of a human being. Your honor's temporary order provided that she have possession of the dog while this case is being litigated, and there's simply no evidence that she's not taking proper care of the dog. If your honor would like us to research the matter further, perhaps both parties could file briefs."

"I'll hear from Ms. Marvel," says the judge.

Michelle's voice is saturated with smugness. She's already won one argument and she assumes she'll win this one. "Your honor, as my client's affidavit sets forth, we have information that Mrs. Hart is only walking Sherman once a day, and that in fact she's often not doing that herself, but assigning that task to the maid. Mr. Hart has always enjoyed walking Sherman—"

"Thank you, Ms. Marvel, you may sit down. Ms. Baynard," the judge says, looking my way, "we appreciate your willingness to be here today. Is there anything you'd like to say about the legal issue?" He motions for me to come to the witness stand.

I know it doesn't matter what I say. My ex-husband has already decided that this dog needs an advocate, and neither Michelle Marvel nor Henry Swinton dares object to having me as the chosen one because they risk pissing me off. Even if they wanted to appeal, the appellate courts are unlikely to interfere at this point, so they're stuck with me.

But I give a little speech anyway because I've done my research. "Thank you, your honor. As you know, for thousands of years, the law has regarded animals as personal property—no different, and even perhaps less valuable, than furniture. This is changing. In the past decade, courts have begun to treat animals as beings with recognizable interests. In a majority of the states, pet owners can now establish trusts for their pets. There are laws in every state against animal abuse. In some states, owners of deceased dogs may claim noneconomic damages—pain and suffering—in malpractice cases against veterinarians. So gradually the law is recognizing what we all know and believe: that animals can suffer, that humans suffer when they lose a cherished pet, and that the relationship between an owner and a pet is qualitatively different than the relationship between an owner and a piece of furniture. While there is still a great deal of controversy over whether courts should use such terms as 'custody' and 'visitation' when dealing with animals, it is not uncommon for judges to approve agreements between the parties to a divorce which provide for the welfare of their pets. And in this particular case, your honor, it's clear to me from my preliminary review of the file that both Mr. and Mrs. Hart love their dog and that they will do anything in their power to assure Sherman's welfare, including cooperating with a guardian to protect his interests." I nod first toward Mrs. Hart, and then toward her husband. They nod back. What else can they do?

Judge Baynard thanks me and orders that I be appointed guardian ad litem "to protect the best interests of Sherman, a miniature schnauzer," that I receive five thousand dollars as temporary fees, to be paid equally by the parties, and that both parties cooperate fully as I investigate the case. He denies Mr. Hart's motion for temporary custody of the dog, but grants him visitation every Wednesday from three to seven and every weekend from Friday at 5:00 p.m. to Sunday at 5:00 p.m.

It's a testament to Joe Baynard's skill as a judge that both parties leave his courtroom looking equally disappointed. As for me, I feel a strange mix of anxiety and determination. I have no idea how to represent a schnauzer, but I remember the photo, those deep-set, dark eyes, and I'm determined not to let him down.

Or maybe, I think as I gather my notes, it's not just the dog I want to protect, but the judge, who looks miserable. Is it this frustrating case? His job? His failing marriage? He motions for me to approach the bench. "Thanks for agreeing to do this," he says to me as the lawyers and litigants for the next case come in. He adjusts his robe, which is too big for him. "You're performing a real service to the court."

I shouldn't, but I can't help myself: "If you have any concerns, your honor, you have my cell number."

For Better or Worse

I've heard it said that women who work together often end up having their periods at the same time, as if their body chemistries shared a secret sisterhood. I suspect this is a myth, but I can testify that for many years my secretary Gina and I were united in our monthlies, sharing both the box of tampons under the office sink and th usual complaints. And about a year ago I noticed her reading an article about menopause at about the same time I was beginning to skip a period every now and then.

Gina and I are both nearing fifty, but our attitudes toward this inescapable fact are utterly different. Gina fights it with all her might. She was queen of the prom at Ashley River High School and first runner-up for Miss Charleston. She's still very pretty—my clients remark on it, especially the middle-aged divorcing males— but various parts of her are beginning to sag and wrinkle despite her constant efforts to prop them up and smooth them over. She goes to the gym three times a week and spends a good portion of her salary on facials and manicures and pedicures, none of which delay the inevitable.

"It's unavoidable," I tell her. But it's easier for me. I've never been pretty, at least not in the startling way Gina is. "You're quite handsome," my mother used to say when I was a teenager obsessing about my flat chest. Her choice of adjectives wasn't helpful. "And your face has such refined bone structure."

At forty-nine I look about the same as I did at forty—a few more gray hairs, a few more wrinkles, but still the same basic Sally Baynard: green eyes, short brown hair, and slim but unremarkable figure. My maintenance is minimal: a haircut once a month, a daily application of discount face lotion with sunscreen, and a lot of walking. I walk to the post office and the court-house when the weather permits, and I walk when I'm angry or sad or frustrated, which means I walk a lot. Gina says the walking won't defeat flabby abs, and she's right, but I can't stand gyms—all those desperate people on treadmills and stationary bikes, running and cycling and lifting weights, driving themselves crazy.

Gina once dragged me to her gym. I was the only woman there in shorts and a T-shirt. Every-body else wore shiny, skin-tight outfits that smoothed their bulges and kept their butts from bouncing as they sweated their way toward the ideal body. "I hate this," I said to Gina. She thought I meant the exercise. I never went back.

I don't want to give you the impression that Gina is one of those women whose devotion to bodily perfection is a sign of a vacuous mind.

38

No. Gina is brilliant. If her mother hadn't steered her into the beauty business at an early age (she was Little Miss something at age five) and brainwashed her into believing that she'd be a movie star (a delusion that ended with a bit part in a B-grade flick filmed in Charleston), Gina might have gone to law school instead of taking a secretarial course at Trident Tech. I taught her how to do legal research, and when she has time she helps me revise my briefs. She also has the ability to step back from the morass of details, to see the big picture with amazing clarity. Whenever I'm dizzy from reading depositions, reviewing accountants' charts, and going over my own notes about who did what to whom, I can depend on Gina to help me make sense of it.

I pay her what she's worth, which is a lot more than the usual secretary's salary.

I've encouraged her to go back to college, then law school. "You could take night courses," I say. "It would take a while, but I'll help you pay for it."

"What's the point?" she says. "I love working for you."

"You'd still be working for me. You'd just be my associate, right?"

"Right," she says, in that voice that means she thinks this is just a pipe dream, not a realistic plan. I'll wait about six months before I bring it up again.

In addition to our clients and our now irregular and dwindling menses, Gina and I have in common our disappointments—maybe I should say disasters—in love. We're different in so many ways, but over the years we've shared these disappointments, comforted and consoled each other. Gina has had two divorces and many more unsatisfactory relationships in between, the sheer number of which I attribute to her determination and eternal optimism. Gina perseveres. She paints her nails and colors her hair. She nurtures her sexuality as if it were a rare orchid.

I, on the other hand, have almost quit trying. I say "almost" because every now and then I feel something that I recognize as sexual. It comes as a surprise, like an old dear friend showing up out of the blue, and I say to myself, "Ah, yes . . ." But it's been a while.

While I haven't been as persistent as Gina, I've had my share of relationships, enough that I've long ago forgotten the complete list of lost loves, but here are the ones I remember:

—The most recent: Ken Smythe, bankruptcy lawyer. I dated him for about six months. Things seemed to be going well—we were going out several times a week—but then he stopped calling and made lame excuses when I called him. I was hurt, but also relieved. His addiction to John Wayne movies (he had the complete collection) as well as his compulsive purchases of expensive boots (he had at least ten pairs) had begun to wear on me.

—Randy McInnis, master carpenter. We had a yearlong romance beginning shortly after he installed new kitchen cabinets at my condo. He was a gorgeous man, blond all over and muscled from his work, but he drank too much and didn't read anything more complicated than *People* magazine. When his response to his mother's death was to "get drunk and screw," I knew I'd had enough.

—Franklin Robard, hotshot Chicago criminal lawyer. We met at a legal conference. He was a little too flashy for my taste—he drove a red Porsche— but smart as hell, with a great sense of humor. We carried on a terrifically exciting long-distance relationship for a while (expensive hotels, room service with champagne), and he tried to convince me to look for a job at a Chicago firm. "Or if you don't want to work, that's okay, too," he said, and I tried to imagine myself as his wife until one night he mentioned that his marriage wasn't "much of a marriage anymore." He'd never actually lied to me. I'd just assumed he was single and available. But when I realized his "proposal" was that I move to Chicago to be his *mistress,* I punched him. He left that hotel room with a wad of tissues over his bloody nose.

—And Joe Baynard, my first real love, with whom I had almost nothing in common other than a law degree. He was Charleston blue blood, the son of a lawyer who was himself the son of a lawyer. I was upstate commonfolk. He went to law school because it was expected of him, I went because I felt a fire in my gut. I wanted to change the world. He was perfectly happy with it the way it was.

So why did we fall in love? There was the physical attraction, but beyond that, I think we were actually attracted to each other *because* of our differences. He was generous with his friendship but not socially adventurous—except in his liaison with me. His law school friends were all from Charleston, people he'd grown up with. Around them he was charming and affable. I tended to be a loner, was opinionated and feisty. He could make me laugh; I could help him see beyond the narrow confines of his world. He mellowed me, helping me to see the other side of every argument, to think before I shot my mouth off. For a few years we were like two halves of one well-adjusted person: we came together, and we fit.

After our wedding, we rented a renovated carriage house behind his aunt's house on King Street, around the corner from his office at his father's firm and within easy walking distance of the county courthouse, where I worked as a public defender. At night we'd come back to the apartment, cook dinner, drink wine, stay up late discussing our cases until we were too tired t talk anymore, then fall into bed and make love. On weekends we hung out with lawyer friends, men and women we'd gone to law school with, or drove up to Columbia to see my mother.

But when I let him convince me to interview at his family firm, things changed very fast. Being a public defender wasn't a career, he said, just a stepping-stone. I still loved my work but the frustrations were mounting: the almost-hopeless cases, unpredictable trial schedule, low pay. "What have you got to lose?" he asked. "Most young lawyers would kill for the chance." So I went for the interview. Of course it was already a done deal. His father showed me the office that was just waiting for a new associate: burnished antique desk, bookshelves already outfitted with the South Carolina Code of Laws, Persian rug. I must have showed some hesitation about the hunting scenes on the walls. "Of course the décor can be altered to your tastes," he said. Joe's uncle bragged about the firm's "commitment toward diversity," which I found odd given the total white-maleness of the twenty-five-member group, but I flattered myself that I would be a trailblazer.

Within a month of my move to the firm, Joe started nagging. Couldn't I be a little more "reserved" around the office, couldn't I avoid talking politics? It's fine, he said, that you want to stay involved in pro bono work, but do you have to take on three no-pay cases right off the bat? In turn, I attacked him for being too subservient to the senior partners—his father and his two uncles, those three bastions of the Charleston bar who inhaled entitlement with every breath and exhaled enough pomposity to fuel an army of aspiring young associates. Our sweet evenings devolved into petty feuding followed by long silences. "Maybe it's time to buy a house," he said. He wanted one downtown, of course. I wanted one on the beach. We were hardly having sex any-more, and I missed a few days of the pill. Still, the pregnancy was a surprise. I kept it a secret, denying even to myself that I might be pregnant, until the miscarriage. "We'll try again," said Joe, as if we'd been trying.

My body healed soon enough, but I procrastinated about going back to work. Joe made excuses for me at the firm. Finally he confronted me: "You hate it, don't you?" I nodded my head. "Then go back to the public defender." I'd never heard him sound so angry.

He was right: I hated the new job, but what I hated more was how I felt about *us*. Those differences that had once attracted us were now constant irritations. The next day, after he left for work, I found an apartment of my own. "It's just a trial separation," I said. Joe begged me to stay—that same "Please, Sally"—but I'd already made up my mind.

Do I regret it? My best friend Ellen asked me that once and I snapped, "Of course not," but the truth is, I'll always wonder if I gave up too soon. My mother certainly thought so. "You had it all," she said, "and you just threw it away." And then, because I was too depressed to argue with her, she kept going: "I never told you this, Sally, but I was amazed that Joe was even attracted to someone like you." Years later she apologized, but her attempts to be supportive about my single life were hurtful: "It will take an extraordinary man to want an independent woman like you."

In the year or two before Mom moved in with me I had a few blind dates arranged by well-meaning friends, occasions on which I realized within minutes of the first handshake that I wanted to go home, where I might rescue the evening with a glass of wine and a good novel. These men were usually divorced lawyers or doctors. We'd meet for dinner, a drink or two, and that would be it. My girlfriends eventually gave up their matchmaking.

And now I have my mother for a housemate. "Are you sure you aren't just using her as an excuse?" asks my secretary Gina, and maybe she's right.

Gina never gives up on love: not for herself, and not for me. She is perpetually panning for a glimmer of gold. And so, when I return from family court after the hearing in *Hart v. Hart* and announce, with a mysterious smile, "I have a new client, and he's really cute!" she springs to attention.

"But I'll tell you about him later," I tease. "Right now I have to review the depositions for the Vogel trial."

"It's been continued," she says. "The clerk just called."

"What?"

"Mr. Vogel's in the hospital. Broken ankle. He'll be okay, but it'll be a couple of weeks."

"Damn," I say, because we'll have to notify a dozen witnesses, but I'm secretly pleased that the three days set aside for the trial are now restored to me. I can catch up on some work, maybe even take a day off.

"So." Gina follows me down the hall and into my office. "Tell me about the new client. How old?"

"I'm not really sure, but not a puppy," I say. I start going through the pile of messages on my desk, pretending to ignore her.

"Look at me, Sally Baynard. I want details."

I laugh. "He's really a dog."

"I thought you said he was cute."

"He's cute, but he's a dog. A miniature schnauzer." And then I explain what my ex-husband has gotten me into.

"You fall for his sweet talk every time," Gina says.

"I'm getting paid for this one, for a change. Guess I should start working on it. Betty's copying the file, but that might take a while. Would you call her and get Mrs. Hart's number, set up a time for me to see her—she's got the dog—maybe sometime tomorrow. Want to go with me?"

"No thanks. Now if it had been a man . . ."

I sort through the stack of phone messages, all in Gina's neat handwriting, dividing them into three piles: Priority, Can wait, Ignore.

Priority: "Rick Silber. Going crazy." Rick is a psychology professor at the College of Charleston. I represent him in his divorce. Did *he* say he was going crazy, or is this Gina's interpretation? I can't tell from the message.

"Richard Silber," he answers. He sounds con-gested.

"Sally Baynard. You okay?"

"I'm holding on, but this is hard to take."

"What's going on?"

"She's got breast cancer."

"Who's got breast cancer?" Is he talking about his wife, Debra, whom he's divorcing, or his girlfriend the graduate student?

"Debra." He can hardly get the words out between sobs. "It's the really bad kind."

"I'm sorry to hear that."

"I want to drop the whole thing," he says. "The divorce."

"Have you talked to her?"

"Not yet."

"How did you find out?"

"Our daughter called this morning. She blames it on me." He blows his nose.

"You can't give someone breast cancer by filing for divorce."

"But how can I . . . how can I proceed with this, when she's . . . God, I'm such an ass."

"Why don't you come in tomorrow morning, we can talk it over?"

"I teach tomorrow morning."

"What about this afternoon?"

"Okay," he agrees, "but I'm going to call her, tell her I'm dropping the whole thing."

"You can't call her. There's a restraining order."

"Can I send her some flowers or something?"

"Don't do anything until we talk, okay?" I looked at my watch. "What about four p.m.?"

"Okay. Sally?"

"Yes?"

"You think I'm an ass?"

Of course I can't answer that honestly. "I think you're upset and confused."

"But, I mean, you're a feminist, aren't you?"

"I guess you could say that."

"So you must think I'm a real ass, running around with one of my grad students, although technically I could argue she's not really a student because she's been working on her dissertation for seven years—"

"We can talk about all this later. Why don't you write down a list of your concerns and questions, and we'll try to address them one by one. Four o'clock."

I open my office window, my free afternoon dissolving into the humid Charleston air. I find myself thinking about the dog. Does he have any idea what's going on between Mr. and Mrs. Hart? Does he suffer? Maybe, but surely nothing like his owners, or like Rick Silber or any of my human clients. And surely nothing like me, the lawyer who listens to their stories, counsels them, soothes them, steers them through the labyrinth of the legal system, around the deep pits of their sorrows, who suffers their angry outbursts, offers a tissue for tears, celebrates their victories and shares their defeats; the lawyer who is—despite her wishful thinking to the contrary—very much like them. For better or worse.

Beauregard's Fancy

You'd think we were headed toward some exotic destination—Bali or Tibet or Kenya—instead of Sullivan's Island, just across the Cooper River from Charleston, but the minute my Toyota starts to climb, I feel the excitement: the arc of the bridge lifts me like a wish. Escape. I'm suspended in a realm of possibilities, no longer earthbound, almost flying.

"We need a little adventure!" I say. My father used to say this all the time. He was always trying to transform the ordinary—a trip to the post office or the hardware store—into something remarkable. It was almost as if he knew his heart would give out too soon, that he'd have to make the best of the life he couldn't escape, the humdrum job at the chamber of commerce, the marriage to a woman who wanted more than he could provide.

"You hear that, Miz Margaret?" says Delores. My mother is terrified if I drive over thirty miles an hour so Delores keeps her company in the backseat. Mom hugs her stuffed chihuahua, which looks almost real except for the miniature sombrero attached to its head. I bought the dog at the hospital gift shop—I was dazed from lack of sleep—during her last bout with pneumonia.

Now whenever we go anywhere in the car, the chihuahua rides with us. He used to sing and play a little plastic guitar, but the guitar fell off, and the battery, thankfully, ran down.

From the top of the bridge we see a big cruise ship heading out through the harbor toward open water. "Look," I say loud enough for my mother to hear, and point toward the ship, but she doesn't seem interested.

Delores, on the other hand, can't take her eyes off the boat. "People got to be crazy to get on those things," she says.

"I have some friends who go on cruises all the time," I say. "They tell me it's very relaxing." I've never been on a cruise, and it's been twenty years since I took more than a few days of vacation.

"If you want to relax," says Delores, "all you need to do is go to Myrtle Beach."

Delores and her boyfriend Charlie go to Myrtle Beach for a week every August. They play miniature golf every morning, and every afternoon they take a dip in the shallow end of the motel pool. If it rains they stay inside and play gin rummy.

Every night they go to a different restaurant, but they always order the same thing: seafood platters with slaw and hush puppies.

I know all this because I once asked Delores how she managed to stay so happy with Charlie year after year. Delores is sixty, Charlie sixty-five.

They've been a couple for twenty years. "'Cause we don't shack up," she explained. "The only time I let him spend the night is when we go to Myrtle Beach. Charlie and me, we have a lot of fun, but a week is about enough twenty-four-hour togetherness."

They go to Myrtle Beach because that's where Charlie grew up, but they never venture onto the beach. "You know how it was back then," she said, meaning when she was young, "no black people on the beach unless they was in uniform."

"But that was a long time ago," I said.

"I don't like the sand in my shoes," she said, with finality, "and I'm not swimming in filthy water with sharks and jellyfish." So I'm surprised that Delores has agreed to spend a couple of hours on the beach this afternoon with my mother while I visit with Maryann Hart and my new canine client.

It's warm for November, almost balmy, and I ignore the thin ridge of dark clouds in the western sky. We've brought an old blanket, on top of which we unfold two plastic chairs. My mother kicks off her shoes almost the minute she arrives. She's always loved the beach. Delores won't remove her sandals, and certainly not her knee-high nylons. "I'll be right over there," I say, pointing to the big white house behind us. "Shouldn't take too long. There's lemonade in the cooler, and cookies."

"Don't worry about us," says Delores. "We'll

behave ourselves. Right, Miz Margaret?" I've told her the "Miz" is unnecessary, but she insists. "You sure *you* going to be all right, yourself? You don't even know that woman. And you ain't too good around dogs."

"I'm okay around dogs."

"How come you ain't got one, like every other single lady in your building?" It's true: it seems that my condo building is full of old ladies with dogs. Even the elevator smells like dogs.

"Don't you think we've got enough on our hands?" I nod toward my mother, who's walking, barefoot, toward the ocean. Delores jumps up, runs after her, and grabs her hand.

My years of lawyering have taught me to size people up within seconds. Most of the time I'm right, but when I'm wrong, I'm not just slightly wrong, I'm way off. So as the door opens and Maryann Hart shakes my hand—hers is small, thin, with long fingernails polished a tasteful pink—I remind myself to distrust my quick assessment: rich, high-born, hasn't worked a day in her life.

There's barking coming from somewhere in the house. "That's Sherman," she explains as she leads me into living room. "He gets so excited when the doorbell rings."

"I'm looking forward to meeting him."

"Yes, well, I thought we might want to talk

before . . . Sherman's so adorable, he can be quite a distraction. Would you like something to drink? I have some iced tea . . . Just make yourself at home while I . . ." Without waiting for my answer she glides off toward the kitchen. I settle on the sofa, the kind that envelops you in its cushiness. The furnishings look rustic but are nearly new, the stuff decorators know how to assemble so that the room looks casual. The walls are full of nice photographs of the island in the old days, sepia-toned, in distressed-wood frames. There are a couple of magazines on the coffee table—*Island Life, Architectural Digest*—but no other signs that anyone really lives here. If I spent two weeks straightening my condo and getting rid of junk, it wouldn't look this neat.

Mrs. Hart comes back with the iced tea. She looks expensive, too, in her ice-blue linen jacket and matching pants, a silk scarf arranged loosely at her neck, silver earrings and bracelet. If she's had a facelift, which I suspect, it's a good one. She's in her early sixties but could pass for ten years younger; only her hands, with those raised blue veins almost the same color as her outfit, give her away.

"This is such a lovely home," I begin.

"You're very kind to say so, but my husband has ruined it for me."

I don't want to get into this, not yet. "How old is the house?"

"The original part—this room—was just a cottage, built around 1920, but it's been added onto over the years, and Rusty and I added the master bedroom suite when we bought it." She sips her tea. "I think it's important that you understand why I . . . why I feel so uncomfortable here." A tear trembles on her cheek. She catches it with her napkin.

"Mrs. Hart, my role is to help the judge decide who should have the dog. It isn't really appropriate for me to get into the other issues in the case, unless they're relevant to Sherman's welfare." As if on cue, the barking gets louder.

"If I told you that my husband and his lover conducted their affair on this very sofa, and that Sherman probably witnessed the whole thing, would that change your mind?"

"Mrs. Hart—"

"Would you expose *your* child to such a thing? Do you have children, Ms. Baynard?"

"Please call me Sally. No, I don't have children, but I've represented lots of kids in court."

"Then I'm sure you have a dog."

"No." I'm beginning to feel defensive.

"Then perhaps," she says, "you can't really understand what I'm going through."

"I understand that both you and Mr. Hart want Sherman to be in the best situation, to be loved."

"I want to protect him from *abuse*, Ms. . . . . Sally."

"Abuse?"

"Emotional abuse. Terrible emotional abuse. You see, my husband—"

"Why don't you tell me about your relationship with Sherman, what you think you have to offer him, and then we can talk about your other concerns." I take out my legal pad. Damn my ex-husband for getting me into this.

She persists. "Yes, of course, but I want you to understand why I'm asking for this divorce, so I'll give you a little background, if you don't mind."

There's no way out. The dog's bark sounds a little hoarse now. I begin taking notes, getting the basic facts.

1st m. for both. Mrs. Hart 63, homemaker.
Mr. H 69, retired president, First Nat'l Bank.

"Do you have children, Mrs. Hart?"

"You said you wanted to concentrate on Sherman."

"Yes, thank you."

"Bear with me, because this is important to the whole question of who should have him." She sighs. "Rusty has had several affairs over the years. I forgave him for all of them except this most recent. So flagrant and tasteless."

"Flagrant?" I repeat as I write this down.

"Yes, that's what I was trying to tell you. It was right here on the sofa. The detective has a video, if you want to—"

"I don't think that will be necessary."

"Anyway, this time he went too far," Mrs. Hart continues. "He brought his little whore into my house."

"I thought . . . Didn't his lawyer say that the, uh, paramour . . . that she's a neighbor?"

"Oh, I don't mean a whore in the *professional* sense, but I'm sure she gets around. All you have to do is look at her." Mrs. Hart runs her fingers through her hair—expertly cut to show off her firm jaw line, colored blond but with a little gray left in so you almost think it's natural—lifting it and rearranging it. She's a woman who knows how good she looks even without a mirror.

> Whore next door: Mindy Greene. 19. College of Charleston drop-out. Drug dealer.

"She's a drug dealer?"

"Well, she hasn't been arrested yet, but it's just a matter of time," says Mrs. Hart. "In any event, as I was saying, I'd been suspecting something, and once we had evidence, we filed for divorce."

"We?"

"Henry Swinton and I. My lawyer."

"Right. And then your husband counterclaimed . . . on grounds of habitual drunkenness?"

"He made that up," she says, a little too loud. The dog raises his volume, too. "I hardly drink

58

at all. Oh, I always keep a bottle of wine on hand in case I have unexpected guests. You should ask *him* how many bottles of bourbon he goes through in a month!"

Mrs. H denies alleg of h.d.
Says H is one w/ drinking prob.

She continues: "I suppose Rusty will say just about anything to win this case. That other thing he said at the last hearing, about my disappearing, that was a gross exaggeration."

I don't remember anything about disappearances, but I pretend to. "What was he referring to?"

"It's just a little local volunteer project. He isn't entitled to know my whereabouts every hour of the day, is he?"

"Mrs. Hart, the only thing that really matters to me is your relationship with Sherman. Why don't you tell me a little about him . . . like, how did he get his name?"

She winces. "Sherman isn't his real name."

"What's his real name?"

"His papers say 'Beauregard's Fancy.' I wanted to call him Beau, but my husband . . . he just kept calling him Sherman, to annoy me."

"Why Sherman?"

"Because when we first got him, he was a little destructive, like the general."

"What did he destroy . . . the dog, I mean?"

"He chewed up the legs of our dining room table. The one downtown. And a couple of shoes. But he was just a puppy. I didn't think it was fair to name such a darling little dog after such a terrible character—and a Yankee, to boot!—but now it's too late." The dog's bark is now more like a bleat, a hoarse plea.

"Maybe you could let him out now?"

"Surely," she says, standing up, walking past me. "He's usually much better behaved. He's been so upset with all of this . . ." Her voice trails off. "*There* you are, my darling. Come out and meet our guest!" But Sherman needs no coaxing. He prances past her, bounds up onto the sofa, and positions himself right next to me. "Sherman," Mrs. Hart exclaims, "Where are your manners? Down!"

"It's okay," I say. He inspects me intently, his dark eyes shining behind white bushy eyebrows, as if he'd like to conduct the interview himself. "I'm not afraid of dogs."

"I'm sure you'll like Sherman. With me, it was love at first sight. Sherman, come to Mommy, darling." The dog settles into her lap and she strokes the top of his head. His ears twitch, then relax. "Rusty—my husband—though, that was a different story. He completely opposed the adoption."

"Adoption?"

"Yes, you know, through one of those agencies

that deal exclusively in purebreds. His first family was just the nicest . . . but the poor woman was diagnosed with pancreatic cancer, so . . ."

"And you say Mr. Hart didn't want the dog?"

"He wanted a bigger dog. So you can imagine how shocked I was when he . . . that he's putting up such a fight over Sherman. Would you like some more tea?"

"No, thanks."

Sherman moves closer to me. His long whiskers brush my hand. "He seems to like you," says Mrs. Hart. "He's not always so good with strangers. That's one of the things I really worry about. Rusty will just let him associate with *anybody*. I feel it's so important not to . . . not to let Sherman just run *wild*. Would you like to see his medical records . . . I mean from the vet?"

At the word "vet" Sherman's ears jerk to attention, then fall back into their relaxed forward curl. "Maybe later," I say.

"I made copies."

"That's very thoughtful. I'll take them with me."

"Though I have to say I'm not totally satisfied with the vet," she says. Yes, the dog's ears definitely rise a little at the sound of "vet." "He was Rusty's choice, the son of one of his old hunting buddies, . . . Tony . . . Oh my mind's gone blank. Starts with a 'B' . . . Brown or something like that. It's in the records."

"What don't you like about him."

"His clinic is way out in the country, on Johns Island. Very inconvenient. I think Rusty chose him just to spite me."

"Mrs. Hart, what are your specific concerns for Sherman's welfare if—and I'm not saying this is going to happen, of course—if the judge were to let him live with your husband permanently?"

"Rusty won't use the leash. Poor Sherman has paid the price with a broken foot."

"How did that happen?"

"A car hit him. It was awful."

"So your husband let him off the leash, and he ran into the road?"

"It's all in the vet's records. And, as I said, Rusty isn't particular about other dogs, he just lets Sherman associate with anybody, no matter how rough." I can't suppress a smile. "You think I'm being overprotective, don't you? That's because you don't have a dog yourself."

"I'm not making any judgments. I'm just trying to understand the situation. I appreciate your honesty, Mrs. Hart. Is there anything else?"

"Rusty uses foul language around Sherman."

"Such as?"

"The 'F' word. And other words. It frightens Sherman. Rusty has an awful temper."

"He yells at the dog?"

"He's abusive."

"Does he hit the dog, Mrs. Hart?"

"Not that I've observed. But he abuses *me*

verbally and emotionally, so I just assume that when I'm not around, he might do something . . ."

"Is there anything else you're concerned about that relates to Sherman?"

"I'm sure I'll think of more later. This whole thing has just been so . . . so upsetting."

"Would you mind if I spend a little time alone with Sherman?" This is what I'd normally do if I were representing a child. I'm desperate for a break from her, and maybe she'll think this is standard procedure—as if there *is* such a thing—in a dog-custody case. "Maybe I could take him for a walk?" Sherman sits up, interested.

"Well, I don't know. He isn't so comfortable around strangers."

"He seems to be doing okay with me. I'll have him back in half an hour."

"Well, if you promise not to let him off the leash, or into the road. Sherman prefers to walk on the sidewalk . . . And he may try to lead you to the beach, but I'd prefer you not do that. He'll get all wet and sandy." She brings the leash, bends over to attach it to the collar. "You have my phone number in case—"

"I won't let anything happen to him."

"Just ring the doorbell when you get back. I don't like to leave the door unlocked."

Sherman walks in front of me, his nose held high. He seems to know how handsome he is: gray

63

coat, perfectly groomed white eyebrows and whiskers. He tugs at the leash and I give him an extra foot or two. At the intersection just past Mrs. Hart's house, he pauses, puts his nose to the pavement, then starts to turn to cross the street.

"No, we can't go to the beach," I say, and give his leash a tug. He looks up at me, black eyes pleading. What harm can come from a little detour? "Oh, okay. I need to check on my mom, anyway." There's a wave of dark clouds coming from the west, moving closer.

The dog leads the way down the public boardwalk through the dunes, stopping to sniff an abandoned plastic bucket and a once-blue flip-flop, bleached by the sun. As the dunes give way to level sand he stops again, sits, takes in the salt smell and the roar of the ocean, then heads for the blanket I brought for my mother and Delores. One of the chairs is still there, but the other has blown down the beach.

"Mom and Delores must have taken a walk," I say. I've always thought people who talk to their dogs are a little pathetic, but I feel the need to explain. "Let's just sit here for a while and—"

It's then that I see Delores at the ocean's edge maybe fifty yards down the beach, up to her knees in the water, arms waving frantically.

"Delores! Where's Mom?" I yell, coming up behind her.

"Out there!" she says, pointing toward the

roiling waves. Sherman hears her panic, lets out a series of piercing barks. "She just wanted to dip her feet in the water. I was holding her hand and then she . . . then she—"

I can barely see my mother bobbing in the waves. She's not exactly swimming—I can't remember the last time my mother went swimming—but floating in the swells, so far out you could mistake her head for a crab trap or a piece of flotsam.

"Mom!" I scream. But of course she can't hear me. The undertow is pulling her farther and farther down the beach, toward Breach Inlet, where even strong swimmers can drown. There's nothing to do but go after her. "Here, you hold onto the dog," I say to Delores, who's crying now. I throw off my jacket, kick off my shoes and jump in—the water's so cold it stings— swimming hard, the waves smacking my face. I see a huge one coming and I duck under, as my father taught me to do so long ago. I come up for breath, go under again, and then I come up next to her.

"Mom!"

The expression in her eyes is not exactly amusement, but something close, as if she thinks it's odd to find another of her kind out here.

"Mom, hold onto me. I'll take you back in." There's an instant when I think she won't listen, but then she grabs my arm. "Don't fight the undertow, just go with it." Slowly, slowly I pull her back to shore, the waves whacking the backs of our heads, half submerging us, taking us under, then pushing us to safety.

Delores meets us with the blanket and wraps it around my mother, whose lips are blue and trembling. "Lord, Miz Margaret, you scared the bejesus out of me. What you been thinking to jump in like that?"

"I lost . . ." my mother says breathlessly. "My dog."

And that's when I realize that we're not just missing my mother's stuffed chihuahua. We're missing Sherman.

How can I go back to Mrs. Hart and say, "I'm sorry, I lost your dog"? As I run up the beach looking for him, the sky turns purple and the wind shoots sand in my eyes.

To stay calm I talk to myself: *You'll find him. How far can he go on those little legs?*

Losing Things

Y ou're always losing things," my mother used to say.

When I was twelve I lost an Easter hat my mother paid twenty dollars for—a lot of money for a little girl's hat back then—a white straw hat festooned with fake daisies and a yellow ribbon that matched my dress. I hated the hat as much as I hated the dress, and maybe that had something to do with my losing it somewhere in the graveyard behind the church. My father was buried in that graveyard, and I used to go there to visit him after the service while my mother chatted over coffee in the parish hall. I believed it was somehow my fault that I had lost him. Maybe I hadn't loved him enough.

And I lost Brownie, the spaniel my father gave me just before he died. He'd adored the dog as much as I had, and in the weeks after the funeral I clung to Brownie as if she had magical powers, as if her presence meant my father hadn't completely vanished from the earth. My mother dealt with her grief by packing Daddy's clothes for the Salvation Army and putting an ad in the paper: "Spaniel free to good home." Weren't *we* a good home? "Of course," she said, "but I'll be working now and you'll be in school. There'll be no one here to take care of the dog." Maybe if I'd cried harder, begged harder, she might have changed her mind, but I was exhausted from weeks of crying. Looking back, I realize she was exhausted, too, and terrified of going back to work after all those years.

And I've lost plenty of cases, important cases—although no case is unimportant for the human beings in the middle of it. Early on, imagining that with a little practice I could be Clarence Darrow, I lost a murder case. I wasn't hoping for a miracle, just for the jury to come back with a manslaughter verdict for my client, a nineteen-year-old woman from the housing project on America Street, who'd shot her boyfriend when she found him screwing her best girlfriend. Surely, I argued, she'd done it "in the heat of passion." There'd be no problem convincing the jury she was only guilty of manslaughter. I hoped they'd overlook the fact that after she discovered his infidelity she drove two miles to her cousin's house to get a gun.

I was young and inexperienced. I shared her righteous indignation. After all, this wasn't the first time her boyfriend had betrayed her with other women, and he'd forged her welfare check to buy drugs. This SOB, I thought, *deserved* what he got. I gave a dramatic closing argument. One of the men on the jury cried. A couple of the women nodded their heads. *Yes,* I thought, *they're with me.*

But the jury deliberated for only half an hour. When the foreman stood up and uttered the words "guilty" and "murder" in a loud, unequivocal voice, I almost fainted.

What had I done wrong? I'd lost my judgment. I'd let myself believe her.

I've lost other cases, of course, but I've never gotten used to it. I always feel I've failed—not just for my client, but maybe for justice in general, although I know that sounds corny. I still believe in justice, though I always give my clients my "Beware of the Notion of Justice" speech.

It goes something like this: *Justice is an ideal we strive for, but it doesn't exist in the real world. The judge who'll hear your case is a real-live, messed-up human being just like you and me, with pimples and prejudices, and on the day she or he bangs the gavel to start your so-called fair trial, she or he may have hemorrhoids or a hangover, or at best will just be in a hurry to move on, to finish up early for that golf game, or a kid's soccer match, or to take a nap. So forget justice. You don't want to gamble your life or your children's future on the temperament of that particular human being. You want to settle on something reasonable, something you can live with. I know, it's not fair. Maybe justice prevails somewhere out there in a different universe, but it's a rare commodity here in the courts of Charleston County, South Carolina.*

I hate giving this speech. I hate the sound of my own voice, the sourness and cynicism in it. But it's my duty to try to save my clients from their own fantasies, their own childlike belief in a perfect world.

Or maybe I'm just steering them—and myself— away from the possibility of another devastating loss. Twice in my adult life I've suffered losses that had nothing to do with the law, losses that knocked me flat, like those giant waves that catch you off guard, roll you over and hurl you onto the hard beach of your own hardheaded self.

After the miscarriage I stayed in bed for a week. Physically I was fine, but I couldn't make myself think about going back to the firm, couldn't eat, couldn't even get dressed. Joe was dealing with his own grief, but he was clueless about mine: "I don't understand, Sally. You didn't want the baby in the first place." Which was true. We'd talked about having children and I'd told him I wasn't ready. But I'd been careless, forgetting to take my birth control pills because in the midst of all our arguing, we were rarely having sex, and after the miscarriage I felt guilty in a way I couldn't make sense of, as if I'd been a bad mother to a child I'd never even met.

Joe was patient, sweet, supportive, but he wanted a child. He wanted a wife who'd have no hesitation about trying to get pregnant again right away. "You'll be a great mother," he said, with too much enthusiasm. Of course he also wanted the kind of wife who wouldn't embarrass him with her politics, her outspokenness, a wife who knew how to throw a fabulous party, who wanted what he wanted: a big house downtown, a comfortable, untroubled life. "My mother can get you in the Junior League," he said, as if he'd forgotten who he was talking to.

Before the miscarriage I'd been considering a separation, but I still loved him, even after all the feuding. He was—and is—a kind and decent man. Afterward, though, I could see with awful clarity how different we were. He deserved a wife who'd make him happy. I deserved . . . I didn't know exactly what, except that it wasn't this uneasy truce.

He cried. I cried. I found an apartment, hired a mover.

And again I was blindsided. How could I feel such grief over the loss of something I'd decided to give up? I've never told Joe about the times—in those first few months after I left him—I thought about going back. I nearly lost my nerve. How would I lead the rest of my life, the next year, even the next few months, alone? I'd looked forward to dinners by myself, eating what I wanted to eat—an artichoke, some yogurt, or nothing at all—but I found I dreaded eating alone. I left the firm and felt a temporary lift at having my old job back again, but soon found my cubicle at the P.D.'s office depressing: those stacks of files crowding the top of the dented metal desk, the swivel chair that screeched when I turned to answer the phone, the torn linoleum floor. I had a new roster of about one hundred clients, but they came with a slew of problems even the best trial lawyer couldn't solve: poverty and poor education, addiction, a string of prior convictions.

After the divorce I drafted a name-change petition to become "Sarah Bright" again, but I never went through with it. I'd established myself professionally as "Baynard" and going back to my maiden name, I told myself, would just complicate things. I carry Joe's name behind mine now, and sometimes it feels like the weight of all my failures in this life, all my losses.

My mother is safe in the car with Delores, wrapped in a beach towel, but there's no sign of Sherman.

I'm drenched, freezing, but I keep running. My breath burns in my chest, but the wind pushes me forward, gives me the impetus to keep going, though there's thunder and lightning now and everyone else has fled the beach. In the distance I make out something on the sand, a creature traveling away from me with a strange, unsteady gait—a desperate dog, I think, a dog who's been hurt—and I run to catch up with it, but when I come closer I see it's just a gray plastic bag filled with wind.

"Sherman!" I yell, but the wind carries the sound of my voice off into nothingness. "Sherman!" I'm not even calling the dog anymore, I'm just screaming.

These Things Happen

I can see in Maryann Hart's eyes what *she* sees when she opens her front door: not a woman, but a girl, a child as big as a woman but a child nevertheless, a wretched overgrown child who's rung her doorbell by mistake, some homeless creature whose wet clothes cling to her angular body and drip onto the doormat.

"I'm so sorry," I blurt out. "I don't know what—"

I expect her to slam the door in my face. Maybe I *want* her to slam the door in my face so I won't have to explain what's happened. I want to run away, back to my office, where I'll draft the order for Joe Baynard to sign, firing me and appointing someone else, some fit and proper lawyer for the dog, someone who's actually capable of walking a schnauzer on a leash without losing him.

But Mrs. Hart doesn't slam the door. "Oh, dear," she says, "That's why I was so nervous about letting you . . . He does this sometimes, with people he's not used to." She's clearly worried, but she doesn't blame or scold. Before I know it she's bringing me a towel, wiping my face, doing her best to calm me down. "Sherman knows his way home. We just have to hope no one picks him up. He's too friendly for his own good."

This is not the same Mrs. Hart I met an hour

ago, so I risk telling her the whole story: how I left my mother and Delores on the beach, thinking they'd have a nice respite from the condo, my mother's unplanned ocean adventure. "I'll drive them home," I say, still breathless, "and come back. Maybe I can find him. He can't have gone too far."

"You're not listening, sweetie," she says. Her "sweetie" sounds at once reassuring and tender. "Sherman knows his way home. He doesn't like being out in the rain, so I'm sure he'll be back soon. You just settle down and I'll make you a cup of hot tea."

"But I need to get my mother home."

"How thoughtless of me! They can't sit out there in the car all wet, can they? By all means, bring them in."

That's how we all end up in Mrs. Hart's kitchen drinking hot mint tea, wrapped in her "old everyday" bathrobes, which seem pretty elegant to me, while our clothes roll around in the dryer. "Would you like something stronger?" she asks. "It's not quite five o'clock yet, but I suppose we could break that silly little rule in a situation like this, don't you think?" There's a wine glass and a half-empty bottle of chardonnay on the counter. Maybe that explains her mood change.

"Tea is fine," I say, speaking for all of us. My mother doesn't seem to care, or even know where she is. "I really am so sorry . . ."

"Don't be silly," says Mrs. Hart, pouring herself a generous helping of wine. "These things happen. You just never know, do you, what life is going to throw at you? Marriage, for instance. Who would think, after forty years . . . but you've been married, right, Sally?"

I'm sure her lawyer told her everything he knows about my marriage to Judge Joe, a story which no doubt included some juicy and fictitious details, now part of the local lawyer-lore. "I was married for a short while, yes."

"And you, Denise?" Mrs. Hart leans forward.

"Delores," says Delores. "No, ma'am. Ain't fallen into that trap so far."

"Trap," my mother repeats. "Trap in the bathroom."

"Do you need to use the bathroom, dear?" asks Mrs. Hart.

My mother shakes her head. "Trap in the bathroom," she repeats. So I have to explain to Mrs. Hart that a couple of weeks ago my mother locked herself in a restroom stall at the restaurant where I'd taken her to celebrate her birthday. For ten minutes I tried to coax her out—"All you have to do is turn that metal lock, Mom"— before I gave up and crawled into her stall from the adjoining one. She didn't seem surprised to see my head at her feet and smiled as if we did this sort of thing every day.

"How awful for you," says Mrs. Hart to my

mother, "but aren't you lucky to have such a devoted daughter? I wish I could say the same for myself."

"I'll get our things out of the dryer," I say.

"You can change in the bedroom on the right, at the end of the hall." Mrs. Hart points the way. The room is dark and cool, decorated in the same expensive-rustic style as the living room. Delores helps my mother while I dress. There are some framed photographs on top of the dresser: a baby on the beach, a young girl—eight or nine—in a Brownie uniform, a color picture of a pretty teenager in what looks like a prom dress. I pick this one up, study it in the dim light.

"Must be her daughter," says Delores, coming up behind me. "Same eyes."

"She doesn't have any children."

"Maybe a niece, then."

I make a mental note to ask Mrs. Hart if she has any relatives who will be testifying about her relationship with Sherman, then remind myself that I probably won't be his lawyer much longer. I can't even be trusted to spend twenty minutes with him.

When we're ready to leave, Mrs. Hart opens the front door to let us out. I apologize again. She gives me a huge hug, a hug I think may be inspired by wine, but it feels good.

And then out of nowhere comes Sherman, his little legs covered with sand, his gray coat wet and matted, and his eyebrows dripping. In his mouth he carries something almost as big as he is—my mother's stuffed chihuahua. He drops it on the porch and then sits and looks up at me, his eyes connecting with mine, steady and calm, as if to say, "What were you so worried about? I found your dog!"

Mrs. Hart picks him up and he licks her face. "You know where home is, don't you, Sherman?" There's sand and mud all over her blouse but she doesn't seem to care.

"She was a nice lady," says Delores as we head back to town.

"Her husband says she's an alcoholic."

"He left her over liquor?"

"She left *him*. She moved out here and left him with the house downtown," I explain. "They own both."

"So if they got two houses, how come they need to bother with a divorce?"

"I guess they're just sick of each other. Anyway, she doesn't want to stay in the beach house permanently. And they're fighting over the dog. The judge is going to have to decide who gets Sherman."

"They could just toss a coin, save themselves a lot of trouble. Whoever loses just goes and buys themselves another dog," says Delores. "If they got two houses, they got the money to buy another dog."

"This dog is like a child to them."

"How long they been married?"

"About forty years."

"If I was the judge I wouldn't let people that old get a divorce," Delores says with great authority. "Seems like you get to a certain point, you been married for almost forever, you shouldn't be allowed."

The Dowager of Domestic Relations

After yesterday's tumultuous day at the beach, my office this morning is a haven of calm until the call from Rick Silber, my (as Gina writes on the message pad) "psycho psych prof." At our last meeting he decided to drop his divorce case, but fortunately I haven't had time to call his wife's lawyer, because now Rick's talked to his daughter, who talked to his wife, and he's not so sure.

"You won't believe this," he says. "I thought she'd be grateful when she found out I wanted to drop the whole thing, but she wants to proceed with the divorce. Said she doesn't want to go to her grave married to me. Her words exactly." There's that tightness in his voice, punctuated by a swallow, that tells me he's holding back tears. "And my girlfriend's left me. So I guess I'm going to die alone."

"You're not anywhere close to dying, Rick." Do I need to remind him that *he* isn't the one who's just been diagnosed with invasive breast cancer?

"I'm forty-five," he says with a sigh. "And I have serious health problems."

"You do?" Isn't he a marathon runner, a health

80

nut who panics if he gains so much as half a pound?

"Yeah."

"I don't remember you telling me about any health problems."

"It's, uh, kind of personal."

"If it might affect your ability to earn a living, I need to know about it."

"It won't affect my job," he says. "It has to do with my sex life."

"Oh." I'm not at all sure I want to hear about Rick Silber's sex life. I know already, of course, that his paramour is a much younger woman, his former graduate student, a fellow marathoner. And I know that if the divorce case ever goes to trial I'll have to bring her in for an interview, get the down-and-dirty, prepare her for a deposition and then for a nasty cross-examination.

"I can't . . . you know, get it up all the time," he says.

"I'm sorry to hear that."

"Yeah, on top of everything else that's going on, it's pretty tough. I've tried Viagra, but it gives me a headache. You have no idea how depressing the whole thing—"

"Rick, listen, I've got a conference call scheduled in five minutes." This is a lie. "And I'm not really the person you need to talk to about this. What about your therapist?" He's been going to his therapist once a week for twenty years.

"You think I'm an ass, don't you?" he asks.

"Of course not, but I think you really need to talk to your—"

"What's the use? My life is totally screwed up."

"Maybe your daughter . . . ," I say.

"I know. You're busy. I'm screwed up and you're a lawyer and you don't deal with the personal stuff."

"That's not fair." I deal with the personal stuff all the time. In the divorce business, there's no avoiding it.

"Sorry," he says.

But now he has me on the defensive. "I can get you in early next week. We'll review everything, see where we stand."

"We did that a couple of days ago."

"But you just told me your wife wants the divorce. So even if you dismiss your complaint, she can go ahead with her counterclaim."

"Sounds like you just want to charge me another five hundred dollars."

"Rick, if you're unhappy with my representation, you can—"

"It's not *you*. I'm fed up with everything. Mostly myself."

"Just call Gina when you're ready to come in again. And in the meantime, we'll sit tight, but you should start working on your answers to those interrogatories."

"Sally?"

"Yes?"

"You're a saint for putting up with me."

I'm no saint. I put up with Rick Silber because he pays my bills. In exchange, he puts up with my bluntness because he knows I'm thorough and I'm tough and I won't rip him off. I'll stand up to bullies on the other side, but won't waste his money bullying back with frivolous motions and outrageous accusations. I won't yell at him even when he's driving me nuts.

I put up with Rick Silber because he needs me. I need him, too, and not just because he pays my bills. The relationship may be dysfunctional, but it works. If you interviewed all my clients you'd have a hard time finding a normal one in the bunch. They're all screwed up. So am I. We're like a big, messy family. Sometimes I hate them, sometimes I love them, but I do my darnedest to help them through their crises, their divorces, and their custody battles.

How did I come to this? How did Sarah Bright Baynard, that fresh-faced idealist just out of law school, the twenty-four-year-old devoted to representing the downtrodden and the unfairly accused, come to be the Dowager of Domestic Relations?

I can't blame it on Joe. Sure, he'd convinced me to leave the public defender's office to join his family firm, but soon after our separation I'd managed to get my old job back. Within a year I was chief public defender, the top job, but after another year I wasn't sure I wanted it. The truth is, I'd run out of steam. I'd work my butt off to save a client, get him probation, only to find him back on the jail list. The first time it happened, I convinced myself it wasn't the defendant's fault. He lived with his mother—an addict herself—on the East Side, in the worst housing project in Charleston. He'd never known his father. He'd grown up right under the Cooper River Bridge but had never even been across it, and though the Atlantic Ocean was minutes away he'd never seen it.

But the second and third times I had a sour feeling in my stomach when I saw the names on the list. I couldn't suppress the feeling that I was being duped. Here I was, working weekends and staying up late on weeknights, to save my clients from themselves. I was giving them my all. Were they reciprocating? Maybe that was the wrong question to ask. In my first stint at the P.D.'s office I'd never asked it. But I was older, more experienced. I needed to feel that all my hard work was actually *changing* something.

I convinced myself that this feeling would pollute my closing arguments, my presentencing speeches, that I was no longer capable of sounding earnest and honest at the same time. I needed to leave the job of enthusiasm to the younger lawyers, the ones who still believed.

I decided to hang my own shingle. I'd have a small, general practice; I'd still do some criminal work, but I'd have more variety: some real estate closings, contract disputes, some estate work, and, of course, some family law—adoptions, divorces, child support, custody.

I got most of my cases through referrals from older lawyers, and most of them hated family law. Divorces were, to them, untouchable. They wouldn't even let those clients through the front door; they sent them straight to lawyers like Sarah Bright Baynard, who'd just opened her practice and was hungry for anything that would pay the overhead. And I had another attribute: I'd just been through a divorce of my own. Somehow, they thought, this made me superqualified to represent the sad, angry, hysterical people who found themselves in "domestic difficulties."

I did not turn them away. I've learned the trade. Occasionally the cases are simple—uncontested divorces, adoptions, name-change petitions—but most of them are complicated, not just because of the emotional issues but because the field of family law has become much more complex. I work with accountants to put a value on businesses and professional practices, with psychologists on custody matters. I love trial work, but I'm also trained in mediation and arbitration.

My clients are doctors and lawyers and business people, about a fifty-fifty mix of men and women.

They aren't all rich. I have my share of teachers, middle-managers, semistarving artists. I'm on the pro bono appointment list and somehow my name seems to come up with greater regularity than other lawyers—maybe because I don't complain too much—so that at any given time I have plenty of "free" clients. Joe Baynard, my ex, has sent a lot of them my way.

I'm sitting at my desk, thinking about *Hart v. Hart*—Sherman, the poor little animal, caught in the middle of the case from hell—when my cell phone rings.

"Sarah Baynard," I say, sounding professional. A lot of my clients have my cell number.

"You got a minute?"

"Joe?"

"I'm out here in your reception area. Brought you something. Gina won't let me come back there without permission from the boss."

"Tell her it's okay." But it's *not* okay. Something's not right. Judges don't just drop in to lawyers' offices. Joe might occasionally stroll down Broad Street to pay a call on his father at the family firm, but he's never stopped at my door, never ventured into the office I rent on the second floor, just a couple of blocks from Baynard, Baker, and Gibson, LLP.

It's been a while since I saw him without his robe, and I'm struck by how much weight he's lost. "Here's the latest motion in the *Hart* case," he says, handing me a big brown envelope, then taking a seat on my sofa without being invited to.

"Oh, I thought that might happen."

"You haven't even looked at it," he says.

"Somebody wants to fire me, right?"

He laughs. "Don't get your hopes up. No, it's about the vet bill. Mrs. Hart wants her husband to pay half. I've set it for next week, thought you might like a heads-up." He's looking around at the artwork on my walls. "You always did like this abstract stuff!"

"Joe, what's going on? You didn't need to hand-deliver this."

"Just wanted a little fresh air. I hate that damn courthouse."

"Well, I'm kind of busy."

"It still makes you nervous to be around me, doesn't it?"

"A little, I guess."

"Ever think why that is?"

"Joe—"

"Maybe it's because you still care a little bit about me." His voice is very soft, so soft I can barely hear him. And then he starts to cry. Hundreds of my clients have sat on this sofa and cried. I've doled out the tissues, an entire forest of tissues. I'm an expert at counseling and calming, but when it comes to my ex-husband's tears I have no professional skills; I just do the only thing that seems right: I sit down next to him and take his hand. We sit there for perhaps two minutes, both silent. Then he stands up and heads toward the door.

"I'm so sorry," he says.

"Have you and Susan been to counseling?" I ask.

"It wouldn't do any good."

"It might. And maybe you should see someone individually."

"I know what I need," he says, squeezing my hand.

"I don't think this is a good idea," I say, pulling it away. Before I can say anything else, he's gone, practically running down the hall toward the elevator.

Gina, of course, is more than curious. "Jeez, he seems kind of frantic. What happened back there?"

"Nothing. He just brought me another motion in the *Hart* case."

"That's weird."

"Yeah, it was a little weird."

"Want to talk about it?"

"There's nothing to talk about."

"Okay, if you say so. Don't forget Mr. Hart, at three. His house."

Lusting in My Heart

The front door of the Harts' downtown house is supersized, mahogany or something, spit-shined so I can see myself in it, with an ornate brass doorknob the size of a grapefruit. I expect a maid in a starched uniform to open this kind of door, but no, it's Mr. Hart himself. "Welcome," he says, without enthusiasm. He doesn't seem grand enough for his house. His flannel shirt is faded and wrinkled, and his toenails have poked holes through his canvas loafers.

I've been inside houses in this neighborhood before, for bar association parties and charity fundraisers, and I've spent many evenings at Joe's parents' home just down the street, but this house is more spectacular than the Baynards'. This is as fancy as Charleston gets, an address any aspiring blue blood would covet. The chandelier in the entrance hall looks like it should hang in a chateau.

Mr. Hart sees me staring up at it. "We pay some fellow four hundred dollars to clean it—three times a year," he says.

"It's magnificent," I respond, as if I need to defend it.

"Hate the damn thing," he growls. He looks at his watch. "You're early. She hasn't brought Sherman yet."

"That's okay, we can talk."

"She's supposed to bring him at three. Want to sit in there?" He points to the room on our right, a very formal-looking parlor with furniture that seems to have been here a long, long time, the kind of furniture that looks like it's never been sat on. "Or there's the piazza on the third floor. That might be better. Nice day. Good view of Fort Sumter. Lemonade or something?"

"No thanks."

I follow him up the wide staircase. He's probably thirty pounds overweight, and at the first landing he stops to catch his breath. "You okay?" I ask.

"Just fat and slow, as my wife would say." We stop several more times before we reach the top. He holds onto the railing, sways a little. "Doctor says I need one of those stress tests, for the heart, but I tell him my old ticker's survived plenty of stress already, it'll probably keep on ticking without the intervention of the medical establishment."

On the piazza we sit in white wicker rockers overlooking the harbor. The view is breathtaking. "Wow, I feel kind of like Scarlett O'Hara up here," I say, though never once in my life have I felt like Scarlett O'Hara. Below us a horse-drawn carriage moves along the street, its driver shouting facts to tourists. Except for the cars, this neighborhood probably looks much as it did before the Civil War—or, as my mother still calls it, the War Between the States.

He hands me binoculars. "We're just down the street from where Mary Chestnut watched the bombardment of the fort. You ever read her diary?"

"No."

"Ought to," says Mr. Hart. "She really tells it like it is. Or was. First night of the war those crazy Confederates sat on their porches—right here— drinking mint juleps, partying while the fort got pounded. Convinced themselves the war would be over in a week, the Yanks would surrender. They should have listened to Petigru."

"Petigru?"

"James Petigru. The lawyer. Stood up at the secession convention and said, 'South Carolina is too small for a republic and too large for an insane asylum.' Brilliant fellow, but nobody listened to him. But I guess you aren't here for a history lesson, are you?"

I take out my legal pad. "You understand my role in the case, Mr. Hart?"

"Want me to be honest?"

"Sure."

"Now mind you, young lady, I have nothing against you, but it seems crazy to me, adding another lawyer into the case. Two is too many."

"I can understand how you feel, but I think Judge Baynard is trying to make sure Sherman's interests are fully protected."

"Would he do the same thing for a goldfish?"

"I doubt many people fight over goldfish."

"But isn't this, uh, this situation . . . unusual? I mean the guardian thing?"

"For a dog, yes. But Judge Baynard has already made up his mind about that, and unless your lawyer can convince an appellate court to reverse the decision before trial—"

"God, no. She's already told me that's not likely to happen. Besides, I'm sure once you've done your work you'll do the right thing, and then Sherman and I can get our lives back to normal."

"Why don't you tell me about that . . . your life with him."

"What do you want to know?"

"Anything you want to tell me."

"Sherman's my best buddy."

"I'm sure he'd be flattered."

"I mean it. Rather spend time with Sherman than anybody I know."

"What kinds of things do you do together?" I sound like a social worker.

"Used to spend a lot of time at the beach together until Maryann decided we were having too much fun out there. He likes to chase shorebirds. Never catches anything, of course, but a man's gotta have hope, know what I mean?"

"How long have you been retired, Mr. Hart?"

"Four, no . . . five years. Good time to get out of the banking business."

"You were president of First National, right?"

"What does this have to do with the dog?" He flicks an insect off his trousers."Sorry, don't mean to be rude. Yeah, I was president of Palmetto State Bank when we got taken over by First American out of Charlotte, which got taken over by First National. The usual corporate gobbling—eat or be eaten. When I started out in banking, I knew every customer by name, knew their mammas and their daddies. If a young couple came in for a mortgage, I'd take care of them, tell them how much house they could afford. If they couldn't afford the house they'd set their hearts on, I'd level with them. I didn't want them getting in over their heads." He smacks his leg, but a fast fly evades him. "You see these mansions all around us? Lots of these people are up to their eyeballs in debt. They borrowed way more than the damn house is worth, and the bank didn't care because, guess what, it knew it was going to sell the note to some outfit, who'd then bundle it with a bunch of other notes, et cetera, et cetera, et cetera. Pretty soon nobody even remembers the idiots who've gotten in over their heads. But then the whole house of cards collapsed."

I nod. "So, you're glad to be out of the business."

"Damn right. Sorry for the rant, but I'm getting around to something: You got any idea what it costs to maintain one of these things? A house like this?"

"I can imagine."

"That's what Maryann does. She *imagines*. Listen, I tell her, here's the deal. You want a divorce, fine, but even if you end up with half our assets, you can't keep this house. It's paid for, but you can't afford to maintain it. Costs close to thirty thousand just to paint it, never mind the taxes, insurance, gardener, pool man, et cetera, et cetera, et cetera. She's asking for alimony, of course, but there's only one pot of money. We were talking about selling it anyway, before all this . . . this nonsense. The judge will understand that, right?"

"Mr. Hart—"

"I'm telling you, even if she gets *more* than half, it won't be enough for her. Jesus, half the queen's treasury wouldn't be enough to keep her in the style to which . . . She hasn't figured that out yet, because she's never had to worry about money, thinks I'm just a damn bank, but let me tell you, this particular old piggy bank—" he taps his chest—"is going to need a bailout soon, and I don't think the government is going to step in to help old Rusty Hart, do you?" He's sweating. "Sure you don't want some lemonade?"

"No, thanks."

"Well, if you want to know the truth, I'd give her most of the money, I'd go live in a damn single-wide, if she'd let me keep Sherman . . . No way she's going to get Sherman."

"That's for the judge to decide, Mr. Hart."

"But you and I both know he's passed the buck, right? You're the one who's going to make a recommendation, and whatever you say, he'll do."

"I'm not allowed to make a recommendation, exactly, just a report on my investigation."

"Okay, a report, but he probably won't have to do too much reading between the lines. He knows how you think. Must have a lot of respect for you, even after you divorced him."

So Mr. Hart knows the history. Of course he does.

I change the subject. "Do you think your wife loves Sherman as much as you do?"

"Maybe. But she doesn't understand him."

"What do you mean?"

"She treats him like a child. All that ridiculous baby talk. It's an insult to Sherman."

"And how do *you* treat him?"

"We're buddies. I respect him."

"You respect him?"

"Sure. He's not just my little plaything . . . Speak of the devil, here they are. Guess we'd better go down."

I follow him downstairs but stand on the front porch as he steps onto the sidewalk and opens the passenger door of Mrs. Hart's huge black Mercedes. I hear shouting.

Mrs. Hart: "Don't you dare let him off his leash . . ."

Mr. Hart: ". . . damn control freak . . ."

Mrs. Hart: ". . . always so irresponsible."

And then Sherman hops onto the sidewalk, pulling against the leash. Mr. Hart slams the car door, hard. As soon as the car disappears he lets Sherman off the leash. "Sit!" he says firmly, and the dog obeys. "Good boy."

Mr. Hart looks back at me. "Want to join us for a walk in White Point Gardens?"

"Sure. That would be nice."

Later, after I've given my mother her dinner, bathed her, and settled her into bed, I make some notes:

> Mr. H lets Sherman walk w/out leash.
> S seems to enjoy playing with other dogs
>   in the park but seems naïve about
>   bigger dogs.
> S is gentle with children.
> Mr. H says he wouldn't want to go on
>   living without S.
> Mr. H denies affair.

He'd laughed when I asked him about that. "Oh, for God's sake, that girl's our next-door neighbor, known her since she was a kid. She's in college now, had some trouble with an economics course. I offered to help."

"But isn't there a videotape?"

"Yeah, Maryann had to go hire herself a detective. He must have been pretty disappointed! The girl came over to the beach house one night while I was living there by myself. She needed help with an assignment. I did my best, though I was never much on the academic econ stuff. Right before she left she gave me a friendly peck on the cheek."

"That's it?"

"She's like a granddaughter. I hope Maryann's detective enjoyed himself, sitting in the bushes, waiting for that little kiss. Bet he'll buy a new boat with what she'll pay him. Don't get me wrong, I'm no saint . . . but this doesn't have anything to do with the dog, does it?"

"I'm just trying to understand the whole situation, that's all."

"Wish I *could* commit adultery, but the old equipment's not . . . Guess you could say I lust in my heart, like . . . who was it? Jimmy Carter? Do me a favor, next time you talk to my wife, ask her where she disappears to for hours at a time."

"Do you think *she's* unfaithful?"

"Would surprise the hell out of me, given her, uh, attitude toward intimate relations, but I've called over there a couple of times, at night, and she doesn't answer. I'm just concerned about Sherman being alone all that time. She can be so damn selfish. Anna used to call her 'Queen of the Universe.' "

"Who's Anna?"

"I've done enough talking today," he said. The look on his face—pained, sad—made me back off despite my instincts. And besides, I was distracted by Sherman, especially when a toddler bounded up to him and pulled his ear. He didn't snap, didn't even bark, just backed away for a moment, then did a kind of dance around the little girl, as if to say, "Let's play some more."

"He's a good boy, isn't he?" said Mr. Hart.

"He is, but maybe we should put him on the leash." There were kids and dogs everywhere, not to mention the cars going back and forth along the Battery. Maybe this was why I'd never had another dog after Brownie—so much responsibility. What if something terrible happened to him?

"If you'd feel better," Mr. Hart said. "Come here, boy. The lady says you've had enough fun for today."

Every case is a story, my favorite law professor used to say. If you want to win, you must tell a convincing story. First, understand the facts, then arrange them to tell your client's story. Remember, you're an artist. The arrangement must be artful.

This sounded like fabrication to me, and I said so.

He smiled. "Ms. Bright, you are ever so idealistic."

"I thought . . . I mean, we can't present perjured testimony, can we?"

"I said nothing about perjury. What I mean to impart is simple: that two lawyers can take the same set of facts and construct two very different narratives. One may emphasize Fact A and use it like a dagger poised at the throat of the defendant. The other may admit A, but argue that Fact B renders it inconsequential. But let me stress something . . ."

You could hear a hundred pens moving across a hundred notebooks. He waited for us to look up. "Don't make the mistake of constructing your story before you have fully mastered all the facts. The premature narrative in your head will interfere with your ability to understand the facts, and that fact you don't know, that fact you overlook, Fact Z, may be the key to the whole case. If you forget everything else in this course, remember that."

A No Win

My friend Ellen Sadler, the prosecutor, is tenacious. She won't let me skip another book club meeting. She dismisses all my excuses like a judge denying a string of frivolous motions.

"My mother doesn't like the night sitter," I begin.

"So ask Delores. She probably won't mind."

"I don't like to ask her to stay late unless it's an emergency."

"Then Mandy will do it." Mandy is Ellen's daughter, a senior in high school.

"You think she can handle Mom?"

"She babysits all the time. If she can handle a two-year-old, she can handle your mother."

"I haven't read the book."

"Nobody cares." Which is true enough. Our group of women, mostly lawyers, has been meeting for at least a decade. We're all avid readers, but the chosen book is just the excuse for conversation that may start with the text but meanders—with the assistance of several bottles of wine—to life, work, war stories, and eventually, just plain gossip.

"What's the book, anyway?" I ask.

"Cormac McCarthy. *The Road*. It's short. I'll send a runner over with my copy if you want to—"

"I read it a couple of months ago. Grim."

"But the relationship between the father and son was so beautifully done, don't you think?"

"Very sad."

"If you want to look at it that way, but I thought it was inspiring. There they are after the apocalypse, starving, and the father is still determined to pass on something good to his son. Anyway, I'll be at your place by six. That'll leave enough time for you to give Mandy the lay of the land."

"I don't have anything to bring for the pot-luck."

"This time we're just ordering in from Beijing Garden."

"But—"

"Six!"

Ellen is the best kind of friend, fiercely loyal but honest when I need that. We went through law school together. She, Joe, and I used to study together. She'd known him since elementary school in Charleston and liked him, but would often tease him about his "South of Broad airs"—she was a suburban girl—and when I told her he'd asked me to marry him, she didn't keep her reservations to herself: "He's a sweetheart, and I can see why you love him, but I just worry that he's going to want you to be somebody you can't possibly be. Maybe you shouldn't just jump right into this . . ."

"What are you talking about?" I'd pressed her,

feeling both insulted and indignant. "He's crazy about me."

"It's hard to explain. Maybe you have to live in Charleston to understand. He just assumes everybody wants what *he* wants, which is basically to live in a nice historic house below Broad Street—which as far as he's concerned is the center of the universe—practice law with his father's firm, and spend weekends at the yacht club."

"You're selling him short. He reads a lot. And he likes to travel."

"And what does he read? *Field and Stream*?"

"He likes mysteries."

"And I don't remember him traveling farther away than the mountains of North Carolina."

"There's nothing wrong with the mountains of North Carolina," I said.

"Yeah, but you'd like an occasional trip to New York, right? And maybe London or Paris?"

"Maybe, but it's not really important. I just want a simple life."

She'd laughed. "You can't be a member of the Baynard family and live a simple life. It's a whole social system and you'll be sucked into it: the yacht club, the hunting weekends down on Edisto, the Cotillion—"

"What's the Cotillion?" I asked.

"That's what I mean! You have no clue! The Cotillion, my dear innocent Sally, is the debutante club. There are others, but this one is THE club."

"I'm way too old to be a debutante."

She laughed again. "Of course you are, but you'd never have been invited, even when you were the right age."

"That's not nice."

"What I mean is, you only get invited if you're from a certain kind of family."

"So, why are we even talking about it?"

"Because Joe's a member, and you'll be expected to go to all the dances. If you have a daughter, I'm sure Joe will want her to make a debut."

"I doubt it. It seems so . . . I don't know . . . antiquated and silly."

"The Baynards and their ilk take it absolutely seriously."

"Well, we're getting way ahead of ourselves."

"You really don't get it, do you?" she said.

And of course I didn't get it, because I didn't want to. I was in love. I was in lust.

At the wedding Ellen was my only bridesmaid. Joe and I decided on a small ceremony with only our parents and a few friends. I thought at the time that this was a good sign, that he didn't really want a big showy wedding, but looking back, I think he wasn't ready to put me on display for the whole Baynard clan. He wasn't quite up to the ordeal of prewedding parties and dinners. So we opted for a civil ceremony in Columbia the day after the bar exam, with a magistrate presiding.

My mother was there, and his parents drove up from Charleston. I'd met them only once, and they were cordial enough, but when they made some excuse about having to get back for a charity event that evening, I felt the chill.

Ellen took me under her wing in Charleston, introducing me to some of the other female lawyers in town. After the miscarriage she hovered over me like a mother (I hadn't told my mother about the pregnancy) until she thought I'd had sufficient time to recover. Then she took me to lunch and locked onto me with those steady blue eyes. "Sally, this is about more than the miscarriage, isn't it?"

And of course she was right. She suggested counseling, but I couldn't see Joe Baynard in a psychologist's office. I'd heard him say, "We Baynards keep our problems to ourselves." No, I told her, we needed some time apart. "It's just a trial separation," I said.

Again she tried to warn me. "Honey, if you leave him, you'll never go back. I know you. So don't kid yourself."

And two years ago, after my mother's diagnosis, when I told Ellen I was moving her in with me "for just a few months until I can arrange something," she was brutally straightforward: "And then what? It's a no win. If you let her stay, you'll drive each other crazy. If you put her somewhere, you'll feel like a creep." Ellen grabbed my hands, squeezed them hard. "You're a strong woman, Sally Baynard, but you're no saint. Do you know what happens to people with Alzheimer's? First she won't remember your name. Then she won't remember *her* name. She'll poop in her pants. Then she'll stop eating."

"I can't put her in a nursing home . . . not yet, anyway."

"You're just trying to make up for all those years you hardly saw her," said Ellen.

"That's not fair."

"It's true."

"I was busy, and she was two hours away. She could have made an effort, too."

Ellen squinted her eyes to let me know she wouldn't let me get away with this. "You're both so damn stubborn."

"She's got nobody else. Anyway, I've already put a down payment on the condo."

"I see you've made up your mind. You can always use an extra bedroom."

And tonight, when Ellen's daughter calls in the middle of the book club meeting (after two bottles of wine but before we've gotten around to gossiping) to say "It's really weird, and I hope I didn't do something wrong, but your mother threw a bowl of Jello on the floor and, like, she seems really upset," Ellen drives me home. She stays until I've calmed my mother down, helps Mandy clean up the mess while I put my mother to sleep with the first three pages of *The Wind in the Willows* (we never get past the first three pages) and stays a while longer to make sure I'm okay.

"Lunch tomorrow," she says before they leave.

"I'll have to check—"

"I know you don't have a trial." She knows this because if I had a trial tomorrow, I'd be preparing tonight, and no amount of cajoling would have gotten me to the book club.

"I need to do some research for the dog case. Maybe next week."

"You can take a break for lunch. I need to talk to you about something. I'll bring sandwiches to your office."

"No meat."

"Right."

In the old days, before there were law schools, my secretary Gina would have been a lawyer. She'd have earned the right to practice law by doing what Abraham Lincoln did: apprenticing, reading the law, studying, drafting pleadings and briefs. This morning she's assembled some cases and articles for me to review, including a survey of U.S. pet owners. Fact: more than half of them would prefer a dog or cat to a human as a companion if they were stranded on a desert island. Fact: Americans spend over 50 billion dollars annually on their pets. Fact: 70 percent o respondents who shared their lives with animal companions said they thought of their animals as children.

Despite all this, the courts have been reluctant to grant pets the same status as children:

> **Bennett v. Bennett,** lst Dist. Court of Appeal, Florida: "While a dog may be considered by many to be a member of the family, under Florida law, animals are considered to be personal property . . . While several states have given family pets special status within dissolution proceedings . . . we think such a course is unwise. Determinations as to custody and visitation lead to continuing enforcement and supervision problems . . . Our courts are overwhelmed with the supervision of custody, visitation, and support matters related to the protection of our children. We cannot undertake the same responsibility as to animals."

Good point. Even if I can work out an agreement between Mr. and Mrs. Hart, will they be able to live with it? I can imagine the continuing spats, the motions filed because one or the other has returned Sherman late, or failed to take him to the vet, and so on and so on. Will Judge Baynard or any other judge of the family court want to spend time enforcing an agreement? And if the case ever gets as far as the Court of Appeals or state Supreme Court, it's certainly possible there'll be a pronouncement like the one in *Bennett v. Bennett*, and a return to the trial court with instructions to treat Sherman as property, no different from a piece of furniture.

And there's another issue I haven't considered—dog support:

> ***Dickson v. Dickson,*** Arkansas: The parties agreed that the wife would have primary custody of the dog, and ordered the husband to pay $150 per month in "dog support." Later the parties stipulated to a modification of the decree: the wife would have sole custody but the husband would have no further financial responsibilities for the pet.

Gina has also found an article from the *Boston Globe* that makes me feel completely inadequate to my task:

> Pet custody disputes have become an increasingly common fixture in divorce cases and [Dr. Anny] Marder, an animal behavior specialist, has consulted in several. To do a proper evaluation, she

likes to spend at least an hour and a half with the couple and the pet. She asks the owners a barrage of questions: which of the two spends more time with the animal, who plays with it more, who feeds it . . . Marder frowns upon so-called "calling contests," a method used by lawyers in some custody cases, in which the owners stand at opposite ends of a room and call the pet to see which way it will go. She prefers to observe the animal's body language as it interacts with its owners . . . Sometimes she recommends joint custody, but only if she thinks the animal can handle it.

I'm no animal behavior specialist. I don't even own a dog. If I can't work out some kind of shared custody agreement between the Harts, if the case goes to trial, I'll have to write a report of my investigation. No matter which one comes out looking better, the other will surely challenge my qualifications and my judgment. I can imagine the cross-examination:

Ms. Baynard, you don't own a dog, do you?
No.
And can you tell us about the last time you had any significant contact with a dog?

Of course this is a question both Henry Swinton and Michelle Marvel already know the answer

to, because by then they will have taken my
deposition.

I had a dog for a while when I was young.

And what happened to that dog?

My mother gave him away.

She gave your pet away?

*Yes. My father died, and she had to go back to
work. She told me she didn't have time for a
dog.*

You were how old at the time, Ms. Baynard?

Twelve.

*Old enough to help with the care of a dog,
wouldn't you say?*

I suppose so.

*So the truth of the matter, Ms. Baynard, is that
your mother gave the dog away because she felt
that neither she nor you could manage the dog,
isn't that right?*

I can't tell you what my mother felt.

*Nevertheless, Ms. Baynard, she determined that
it was best for the dog not to continue to live in
your household, correct?*

*It was a very difficult time. My father died
suddenly, finances were tight, and my mother had
to go back to work.*

Did you love your dog?

Of course. I adored him.

*And if you don't mind my asking, Ms. Baynard,
how old are you now?*

Forty-nine.

So it's been thirty-seven years since your mother gave your dog away, and in all those years you've never had a dog, is that correct? In fact, you've not owned any other kind of pet during all that time!

I shared a kitten with my roommate in college.

You shared *a kitten? What exactly does that mean?*

She was a stray. We fed her.

And what happened to that cat?

At this point, I imagine, I turn to Joe Baynard, desperate for him to put a stop to this, but he's not paying attention.

She ran away.

So you are asking the court to accept your report as to Sherman's welfare, based on this paltry experience with animals, Ms. Baynard?

I'm safe in my office now, not sitting on the witness stand in family court, but I can feel sweat collecting on my forehead, the hot tide of panic rising from my neck to my cheeks. I can come up with lots of excuses why I've never had another pet. After she gave Brownie away, though I begged, my mother said, "No more dogs." In college, at USC, no animals were allowed in the dorms. Then there was law school, when my classes and studying and part-time job took all my energy.

After I moved to Charleston, newly married, I

111

was too busy learning how to be a real lawyer. Joe wanted a dog. His uncle bred Boykin spaniels, spirited hunting dogs with silky brown coats. We could have our pick of the next litter, he said. Maybe next year, I said.

After we separated I came close. I thought it would be nice to come home to a dog instead of the empty apartment. I even checked out a book from the library, *Choosing Your Dog: A Hundred Popular Breeds*, and perused its pages, trying to imagine myself with a standard poodle (but so much grooming!) or a golden retriever (too big!) or maybe something smaller, maybe a terrier (too feisty?). "Don't obsess over it so much," said my friend Ellen. "Just go to the shelter, pick a dog you like. It isn't so hard, really."

Then why did it seem so hard? Was I really so much busier than other people? Or was I afraid I wouldn't be able to be a decent pet-parent? Afraid to commit to a long-term relationship? Now I have another excuse: my mother. Still, I feel my doglessness is somehow indefensible, a defect that indicates some deeper character flaw.

Gina comes back to my office to remind me that Ellen is coming in five minutes. "You gotta read that case from Tennessee," she says. "Where the wife said she should have custody of the dog because she would keep him away from . . . how did she put it? 'Ill-bred bitches.' And she took him to her weekly Bible class. The husband, he said he should have the dog because he'd taught him some good tricks, like riding on the back of his motorcycle."

"So, who won?"

"Joint custody, with the dog moving every six months. But then the wife moved to Texas, so it was a real mess."

"This is giving me a headache."

"You'll figure it out. You're a great lawyer, so you'll be a great lawyer for the dog. Hey," she smiles wickedly, "I like the sound of that. Maybe we should change your sign outside: SARAH BRIGHT BAYNARD, J.D., LAWYER FOR THE DOG.

No Secrets

"I meant to tell you this on the way home from the book club meeting, but the Jello emergency got in the way," says Ellen. We're having lunch in the room that doubles as my library and conference room. I have to move several stacks of papers to one side of the table—ongoing research projects, appeal briefs, depositions waiting for review. Thank goodness Gina knows where to find things, including the files I sometimes leave in the trunk of my car.

"What's up?" I ask Ellen.

"I don't want to complicate your life . . ." she begins, ". . . but I thought you should know. It's about Joe."

"*My* Joe?"

"Well, if you want him, I guess." She laughs.

"I didn't mean it that way."

"Maybe you did."

"Stop."

"Okay, I guess you don't want to know any more . . ."

"But you're going to tell me anyway, right?"

"I won't force it on you," she says.

"Like hell you won't."

"Whoa, girl. You're still pretty raw after all this time, aren't you?"

"I'm not raw, but I don't understand why you came all the way over here to tell me something you could just as well have told me over the telephone."

"Just thought you might want to talk about it," Ellen says through a bite of her sandwich.

"What's there to talk about?"

"Don't you want to know the gossip?"

"Not really." But of course I do.

"He left Susan."

"I heard they were separated." Why am I being so cagey with my best friend?

"I guess it's out, then."

"Another woman?"

"Not the Honorable Joseph Henry Baynard III. In a way, though, it's even worse. The idiot tells Susan he's in love with someone else. He tells her he hasn't *done* anything, but he's in love. He actually asks her to help him 'work through it.'"

"That went over well, I'm sure."

"Yeah. She went ballistic. And of course you know who everyone thinks the other woman is." Ellen smiles a wicked smile, as if she's caught me.

"I have no idea."

"Oh, don't pretend to be so dense."

"Stop it!" The sound of my own shouting shocks me.

"Oh, honey . . . I didn't realize . . ." Ellen drops her sandwich, comes around to my side of the table, and bends down to hug me. "I thought you . . ."

"You thought what? That I'd be delirious with joy?"

"I thought you'd want to know. Haven't you wondered why he got you involved in that dog case?"

"He's appointed me on lots of cases. All the judges appoint me. It's a pain in the ass, but I do a good job."

"But this case . . . He went out of his way to give this dog a lawyer."

"The case is tying up his court. He's hoping I'll help settle it."

"You aren't thinking rationally. If the case is really driving him crazy, why would he insist on hearing all the motions himself? He's the administrative judge, he can assign the motions to other judges, but instead he's keeping the whole case for himself."

"I hadn't really thought about it. Maybe because it's such an unusual case?"

"That's bullshit, and you know it. He's still in love with you and he knows if he calls you and says, *Sally, I'm still in love with you and I need to see you,* you'd tell him you're not interested, so he involves you in the case from hell, gets you into his courtroom for a dozen motion hearings and a trial and then, who knows . . ."

"He doesn't need to play games like that," I say. "He was just here yesterday, as a matter of fact . . ."

"What?"

". . . but he didn't say anything about being in love with me."

"The man has *some* pride," Ellen says. "What was he doing here, then?"

"He was delivering a motion that was just filed."

"Right."

"I know, it was pretty lame, but I just think he's going through a bad time. He's having a mid-life crisis, not thinking straight."

"He told his wife he's been in love with you since the divorce. He never *stopped* loving you, in fact."

"What an idiot," I say, but I feel something I haven't felt in a long time. I push it away. It's too dangerous.

"And after he confessed, like the gentleman that he is, he moved out the next day."

"Where are you getting your information?"

"She told her sister, and her sister's best friend is my—"

"Never mind. If it's true, he'll get over it. They'll work things out. They've been together for what . . . sixteen, seventeen years? What about the kids?"

"The boys are away at some boarding school. The same one Joe—"

"St. Paul's."

"Yes."

"He had no right to involve *me*. There's nothing going on between us . . ."

"He made that clear to her. But of course she doesn't believe him. Looking at the case from her point of view—"

"It isn't a *case*—"

"Okay, looking at the *situation* from her point of view, you're already involved. Maybe it was a long time ago, but it's not as if the whole thing is a figment of her imagination, is it?"

"So, I'm innocent, but I've already been convicted."

" 'Innocent' might be a stretch," she says. "You'd better stick with 'not guilty.' There's a difference."

We finish our lunch, quiet for a while. Then she looks at me with those unwavering blue eyes of hers. "You haven't really said how you feel about him."

"I feel sorry for him."

"That's all?"

"That's *all*." But she knows I'm lying. The truth is, I don't understand what I'm feeling. I just know it's dangerous. "I guess I need to get out of the dog case."

Ellen looks at me suspiciously. "Assuming you want to discourage him."

"Of course I do. I'll make a motion to be relieved."

"You think you can put this on the record?

118

Your honor, I move to be relieved as guardian ad litem for the dog because it has come to my attention that you are in love with me. No, that won't work. Where are you so far, in the case?"

"I've reviewed the pleadings, interviewed Mr. and Mrs. Hart, spent some time with the dog, done some research. I'm driving out to talk to the vet this afternoon."

I can practically hear the gears shift in Ellen's brain. "Yeah, interview the vet. Get him to say that all this back and forth—this split custody—is bad for . . . What's his name?"

"Sherman."

"Right. Get him to say that Sherman, like all dogs, needs consistency. Then maybe you can move to bifurcate, get an expedited trial on the issue of who gets the dog. Yes, that makes sense: a short trial on the dog issue, which would be separate from the rest of the stuff, the property division and alimony and all that. You only need to be involved in the dog issues. It'll save the parties money, too, since they won't be paying you to sit around through hours of depositions and days of trial."

"That's a good idea."

"But you realize this doesn't solve the whole problem," Ellen says. "It just gets you through this one case sooner. Limits your exposure to Joe, assuming that's what you want."

"*Of course* it's what I want." But I can't look her in the eye.

"I hate to bring this up," Ellen says, "but you haven't done anything to encourage this, have you?"

"Absolutely not."

"No secrets from me, right?"

"No secrets."

"Because you know you can talk to me."

"Ellen . . ."

"Okay, okay." She stands up to go. "I forgot to ask . . . What kind of dog is it, anyway?"

"Miniature schnauzer. Very cute. Smart, too. Want to see a photo?"

"Sounds like you're falling in love."

"He's a nice dog, but it's still crazy for them to fight over him, don't you think?"

"I'd fight over Hershey."

"Come on, you mean it? He's a dog, not a child."

"Tell you what, Sally Baynard, you get yourself a dog, let him work his way into your heart for a couple of years, then try to imagine life without him."

Not Too Much Pressure

If you're a woman past forty it's risky to look at yourself in the rearview mirror, especially on a late afternoon when the slanting sun accentuates every wrinkle. Who *is* that woman? I never get used to seeing her, the one who pretends to be me.

The real me, the one I always expect to see, is about twenty-five. Her eyes are clear and bright, so green they startle you. Those eyes are brimming with energy and optimism, as if there is nothing she can't do, nothing she can't handle.

My friends say, "You look great for your age," and yes, I still have the nice thick brown hair (with only a few streaks of gray) and the good skin and the trim figure (okay, the thighs could use a little work), but I'm not that spunky woman who graduated from law school second in her class, ready to fight for the rights of the underdog, that woman who had as much heart as brain, and who would give it all for what she believed in—including Joe Baynard.

She didn't disappear all of a sudden; it's more like she dissolved little by little, so slowly I hardly noticed—like an old color photo gradually fading until one day you can't see it at all—and yet I still expect to see her when I look in the mirror.

This afternoon, as I drive to the vet's office, I try to let her go, try to concentrate on the traffic. It's bumper to bumper across the Ashley River and down Folly Road, but it eases up after I cross the Wappoo Cut and turn onto Maybank Highway, over the Stono River Bridge and then onto Johns Island.

The island isn't what it used to be. The developers have chopped up the old farms, turned them into places with faux antebellum houses and ostentatious names—"Palmetto Plantation," "Eagle Landing," "The Estates at Mackay's Point"—but eventually these give way to stubbled fields and brick bungalows, rundown roadside restaurants. *Turn right at Buzzy's Barbecue,* he'd said, *and come on down about a quarter mile. You'll see my building, one story, concrete block, kind of beige. I should be finishing up about five.* The sign out front, VETERINARY CLINIC, is small and plain, a sort of anti-advertisement, half-hidden behind a bush.

Inside, the smell of disinfectant can't mask the odor of animal, a rich olfactory mix both ancient and fresh, that seems to have permeated the whole place. I imagine the thousands of dogs and cats who've come and gone in this place, the young and healthy who were brought for their shots, the injured and sick and old, the ones who'll be put to sleep, but this close to closing time there's only one dog—a dachshund—

who jerks against her leash when I come in.

"Hillary! Sit!" says the owner, a woman slumped in one of the green plastic chairs as if she's been here a while.

The receptionist slides the glass window open when she sees me. "You're Ms. Baynard, right? He's with an emergency right now, and then he's got one more patient."

"Fine," I say, though I'm annoyed. The stack of magazines isn't promising: *Cat World*, *Sporting Dog*, *Able's Veterinary Supply*, and *People*.

The woman with the dachshund leans toward me. "Here, I'm finished with this one," she says, handing me a catalogue, *PetStuff*. "It's old, but they got some neat things in here."

"Thanks."

"You picking up your pet?"

"No." I don't want to tell her I'm a lawyer. That can be dangerous, because the next question will be, *What kind of lawyer?* And if I tell the truth, *I wonder if you'd mind answering a question? I have this girlfriend who's not happy in her marriage* . . . It's amazing how many girlfriends have trouble in their marriages.

"Dr. Borden's been taking care of my Hillary for years. He's just the sweetest, kindest man. So sad, what happened."

I have no idea what she's talking about. I flip through the catalogue. There's a dog ski jacket on sale for $39.95. Pink or blue. I wonder what kind of person buys a ski jacket for a dog.

She continues: "His ex-wife moved to California, took their son. The doc hardly sees him anymore."

I'm about to mumble a noncommittal answer when the receptionist calls out, "Hillary, we're ready for you." The dachshund jumps to attention, then remembers where she is and freezes until her owner coaxes her through a door leading back into the clinic.

I open my briefcase, get out a legal pad, and start a to-do list.

Work:
Prepare for Vogel trial
Draft motion to bifurcate in *Hart v. Hart*
Send out discovery requests, Silber case
Schedule meeting of Pro Bono Committee
Revise Follett brief
Write letter to J. Johnson re: past due bill

Other:
Schedule Mom's appt with Dr. Payne
Refill prescriptions
Call dishwasher repair guy
Haircut
Dry cleaning

I keep a to-do list on my phone, but it's always so long that it discourages me. This handwritten list seems less threatening, though I always feel there's something I'm forgetting.

In the early days of her Alzheimer's, my mother kept lots of lists. When she started to include things like "brush teeth" and "wash face" I knew there was something really wrong. And then she began to lose the lists. I'd try to console her: "Mom, don't worry about it. If you forget something, I'll remind you." But she panicked. She'd roam from room to room, tearing through piles of papers, looking under magazines, even through the underwear in her dresser, for the lost lists. She'd cry. Sometimes she'd scream. That's when I hired Delores.

The receptionist opens her window again. "I'll be leaving now," she says. "But he shouldn't be much longer. You want a Coke or some water or something?"

"No thanks." I look at my watch. I've been here an hour already.

I go back to the catalogue, skim through the pages of dog food choices, move on to the toys. There's a "bone" that floats on water, a special line of "fitness toys," and then a page of Martha Stewart toys for pets. "Unbelievable!" I say aloud, just as the vet opens the door. He looks exhausted, his blue scrubs covered with stains and animal hair.

"I told you that stuff is really neat, huh?" says the lady to me. "If you go online you can get coupons." Her dog is eager to leave the clinic and pulls her out the door.

"Sorry you had to wait," says the vet. "Just give me a minute to wash up and change."

"No problem."

He comes back in a plaid shirt and blue jeans. He's tall, trim. "I haven't eaten all day. Mind if we talk over dinner?"

I've already arranged for the night sitter to take over when Delores leaves. "Okay."

"There's a pretty good seafood place not far down the road."

"That's fine." No need to go into the vegetarian thing.

"I can drive you over there and bring you back. Provided you don't mind a messy truck." It's an old pickup. "Just throw your stuff in the backseat. You might have to yank on the seat belt a little." I feel way overdressed in my black suit and matching black heels. "The place has great fried oysters," he says. "Only trouble is, you have to watch where you park. At high tide half the parking lot goes under."

He turns onto the main road for maybe half a mile, then we bump along a rut-ridden dirt road that winds over the marsh. "Sorry about the shocks. Truck's not much to look at, but it's dependable. And my girls like to ride in the back."

"How old are they?"

"Six and seven. Susie and Sheba." He laughs. "Oh, you think . . . no, they're retrievers. Here we are." He comes around to open the door, takes my hand to help me down. "Watch your step. It's a swamp out here."

Inside the place looks more like a fishing shack than a restaurant: four or five tables covered with red-and-white canvas tablecloths, a hand-drawn sign, RESTROOM OUT BACK, but it's clean. We take a table near the window over the creek. When I order a salad, the waitress looks at me as if I'm an alien.

"You can't come here unless you try the fried oysters," the vet says. "Best seafood in Charleston County. Right, Caroline?"

"Right, Doc."

"Okay, I'll try them." At least it's not beef.

"Fries or baked potato?"

"Baked potato, please."

"Beer, Doc?" asks Caroline.

"Sure." He looks my way, "What's your pleasure?" He gestures toward the sign over the cooler which lists, along with the seafood offerings, the beverage choices: iced tea, coffee, a selection of beers.

"I have to drive home."

"Don't make me drink alone."

"A Dos Equis, then."

"We're outta them," says the waitress.

"Then bring us a couple of Coronas," he says.

"None of them today, either."

He orders two Buds, and when she leaves he leans toward me. "I always forget. The beer list is a fiction. It's Bud or Bud Lite. Unless they're out of Bud Lite." He brushes a stray strand of hair off his forehead, and even in the dim light of the restaurant I can see how nice his eyes are, brown, deep-set, behind glasses held together with a safety pin at the temple. "So, you said you had some questions."

"You understand what my role is, right?" I say.

"I think so, but this is the first time one of my dogs has had a lawyer!" He smiles, but even with the smile there's something sad about him.

"It's the first time I've served as lawyer for a dog, so we're even."

"I guess I shouldn't say *my* dogs, but I feel like they're all mine, in a way." He plays with his paper napkin, unfolding it, folding it. Maybe he's nervous around lawyers.

I take a sip of my beer. "This is a lot like a custody case, or at least Judge Baynard is treating it like a custody case. He—"

"Baynard. Any kin?"

"Distant." I don't want to explain. "Anyway, the judge is treating this like a child custody case, despite the fact that in South Carolina the law is pretty clear that a dog is just property, like a piece of furniture."

"Well, Sherman's a good deal livelier than a piece of furniture."

"He certainly is. But what I'm trying to say is that I don't have any experience representing animals, because as far as I can tell this is the first time any court in South Carolina has appointed a lawyer to look after the best interests of an animal. There aren't any precedents except from other states."

"I'm sure you'll do fine." I like the sound of his voice, reassuring without being condescending. The waitress brings our food. I start with the baked potato, a few bites of slaw. "Don't let your oysters get cold," he says. "They're fresh, right out of the creek."

I cut an oyster in half, take a bite. I'd forgotten how good fresh oysters can be. After I left Joe I embarked on a routine of self-purification—maybe self-punishment—running five miles a day, going vegan. I've since given up the running and compromised the veganism with eggs and cheese. I've stayed away from meat and even seafood, but these oysters remind me of good times, of Sally Bright Baynard with the lively green eyes and an appetite for life. They're succulent, salty with a hint of sweetness. "So if this were a child custody case, I'd talk to the pediatrician, and I'd arrange for a psychologist to interview the child and the parents. In this case, you're kind of like the pediatrician and the psychologist all rolled into one."

"Never thought of myself as a psychologist. I take care of some neurotic animals, but it's usually because their owners are a little crazy themselves." He laughs. He's relaxing now, and so am I.

"Do you have a copy of Judge Baynard's temporary order?" I ask.

"Mrs. Hart told me about it."

"What do you think about the schedule? It seems to me like there's a lot of back and forth for Sherman."

"He's a spunky little guy. He can cope with it."

"The Harts seem to have very different styles of parenting."

"Yeah," he says, wiping a spot of sour cream off his lower lip. "Rusty's pretty laid back. Maryann's a little uptight. But they've always been a good team, at least for Sherman."

"But they're not a team anymore."

"True."

"If you had to choose between them, could you do that?"

"I'd hate to. You need me to decide that now?"

"No, we have some time."

"Want dessert? Coffee?" he asks. "They have some great blackberry cobbler."

"Just coffee, thanks. Anyway, I think it would

be better for Sherman not to delay a final decision longer than absolutely necessary."

"He seems to be doing okay," the vet says. This isn't what I want to hear.

"Judge Baynard will probably go along with my report, and I'll probably go along with what *you* recommend."

"You think I'll have to testify?" He looks worried. "I try to stay away from courtrooms."

"If the case goes to trial, you'll have to testify."

"Any idea when that will be?"

"Well, a case like this, with significant assets, the alimony issue, and question of who gets Sherman, could take six to nine months, maybe longer, to get to trial. And before that they'll take your deposition, and there'll be a number of pretrial motions."

"Wow, I had no idea."

"Divorces can be really complicated when they're contested."

"I wouldn't know," he says.

Normally I'd let this drop, but the beer makes me curious. "I thought someone told me you were divorced."

"Yes, but I didn't want to fight." He swallows. "I let her have pretty much everything except the clinic."

I can tell he's uncomfortable. "Sorry. It's none of my business."

"So, you were saying it could take six to nine

months before the case goes to trial. Maybe they'll settle. Don't most of the cases settle?"

"Yes, but this one doesn't seem likely to. At least that's my impression after talking to both parties. They've already been to mediation and that didn't work. But I have an idea about how to move it along faster and keep your involvement to a minimum. I can make a motion to bifurcate."

"What does that mean?"

"If the judge grants the motion, the trial would have two parts. The first part would be restricted to the question of what's going to happen with Sherman. That would probably take half a day or so, a day at the most. Then once the judge makes a decision about who gets him, the Harts will probably settle the rest of the case. At least that's my gut feeling: what they're really fighting about is the dog. Without a bifurcation, the trial could take weeks."

"Weeks?"

"Yes. Of course, you'll only be there for your testimony, but I'm looking at the whole situation and trying to figure out what's best for Sherman. The sooner the case is over, the better for him."

"I never heard of this . . . what is it? Bifurcation?"

"It's sometimes done in divorce cases that involve child custody," I explain. "It can prevent the parties from using the kid as a pawn to get some financial advantage. And once the judge decides who's going to have custody, often the parties settle the rest."

"Sounds reasonable," he says.

"So I'd like to get an affidavit from you, to the effect that it would be in Sherman's best interest to resolve the custody question without delay. Which means you'd have to point to some adverse effect this back-and-forth is having on him."

"So far he seems okay."

"You've seen him several times since the Harts separated, right?"

"Twice, I think. It's in the records. You've got copies?"

"Yes, but they only indicate when he was brought in, not who brought him, and what you treated him for. Can you give me more detail?"

"Maryann brought him in for a skin condition. He was scratching the hell out of himself. She blamed it on Rusty, said Rusty had let him eat table scraps. Asked me to call Rusty, which I did, but not because of the table scrap thing. I just wanted to . . ."

"Get her off your back?"

"I guess you could say that. Anyway, it turned out she'd started using some fancy perfumed shampoo. Sherman was probably allergic to it. And then there was another time recently, Rusty brought him in for a general check-up. Said he seemed more low-energy than usual, kind of depressed. I examined him, didn't find anything. I suspect Rusty is the one who's depressed."

"Who usually brings him in to see you?"

"When he was a puppy, Maryann did, for his core vaccines and wormings. Lately more fifty-fifty, I guess. Early on, Rusty brought him in for the broken leg."

"How did that happen?"

"He got hit by a car."

"Mrs. Hart blamed Mr. Hart for letting him off the leash, right?"

"But that might not be what happened. Rusty told me they were crossing the street. Sherman was on the leash, but some kid took a corner too fast, didn't see the dog. Maryann was pretty upset, said Rusty was always letting Sherman run wild. Rusty was upset himself, but maybe it wasn't his fault. You sure you don't want some cobbler?"

"No, thanks. I'm stuffed. So, about this leash thing. I don't know much about dogs . . ."

"I can tell." He smiles.

"How?"

"I don't know . . . Just a hunch, but I guess I shouldn't jump to conclusions. Dog people are all different. Take Rusty and Maryann Hart. They have completely different philosophies about Sherman, but they both love him, want the best for him. And in their own ways, they're each good for him."

"But back to the leash," I press on. "Mrs. Hart insists he shouldn't be off the leash. Is she right, or just overprotective?"

"Sherman's well-trained, but I recommend that dogs be on the leash when they're near traffic or around other dogs. The problem with schnauzers is that they'll take on bigger dogs. They aren't particularly aggressive, but they're curious, and sometimes they'll provoke a fight without meaning to. So to be safe, I'd say yes, he needs to be on the leash when he's outside."

"So she isn't overprotective?"

"No, I wouldn't say so. She can come across as a little silly sometimes, but she's very committed to doing the right thing for Sherman. But, like I said, so is Rusty. They just have different approaches."

I look at my watch. "One more question. There's a motion next week about your bill. Mr. Hart wants Mrs. Hart to pay your fees."

"Yeah, Rusty told me. Says he's paying a lot of alimony, so she ought to use some of it to pay me. I'd rather stay out of the financial stuff."

"How much do they owe you?"

"A little over five hundred dollars, I think, but it's no big deal. They always paid on time before this divorce. I figure this is just a power struggle. They'll pay eventually. I don't want to get involved in their skirmishes over money."

"I don't blame you. I just want to make sure

you won't stop taking care of Sherman before the case is resolved."

"I'm a patient man," he says.

I look at my watch. "I have to get home."

"Children?"

"No. My mother lives with me. It's a long story, but I have to get home to relieve her sitter." The waitress brings him the check. "Let me get this."

"I invited *you*."

"I insist."

"Only if you let me do it next time," he says.

Outside it's already dark. "Watch your feet," he warns. "Tide's starting to come in. And next time don't wear such nice shoes." There it is again: *Next time.*

On the way back to his clinic I press him some more about the affidavit. "Can you say it would be better for Sherman to get this custody issue over with, so that he won't have to go back and forth?"

"Well, I can't really say he's suffering."

"You don't have to. Maybe that it would be better for him to have a stable routine? I mean, would you ever recommend this kind of arrangement as a permanent thing?"

"No. A dog needs to know where home is."

"So, if it isn't a good idea permanently, it isn't a good idea even on a temporary basis, right?"

He pulls into his parking lot, turns to me

smiles. "You're persistent, aren't you? Okay, draft something and I'll look it over."

"Fine."

"You want a nice dog?"

"What?"

"I've had this one a couple of months now. Owner isn't responding to letters or phone calls. I could call the shelter, but . . . She's just a really special one."

"My place is small . . . And I have my mother."

"Your mother doesn't like dogs?"

"She has Alzheimer's."

"Alzheimer's patients do really well with dogs. Why don't you let me bring the beagle over sometime, you keep her for a few days, just for a trial run?"

"I don't know . . ."

"If it doesn't work out, I'll take her back. You can't lose."

"I'll think about it."

"Give me a call when the affidavit's ready," he says.

We shake hands. I like the feeling of his around mine—warm and comfortable, not too much pressure. I like the idea of *next time*. But then I scold myself: *You're the lawyer, Sally, and he's the witness. Let it go.*

Dogs Can Tell You Things

By the time I get home it's after eight and Vicki, the occasional night sitter, is upset—not because I'm late, but because my mother has been crying.

"She wouldn't touch her supper, but later she tried to put one of those fake apples in her mouth, and when I took it away from her, she called me a whore."

"She doesn't know what she's saying."

"Actually, it was 'fat whore.' At least she got the 'fat' part right." Thank God Vicki's got a sense of humor. "Maybe you ought to get rid of that fruit," she says.

I bought the fake fruit soon after I moved into the condo, trying to make the place seem more homey. Plastic apples, lemons, limes. They look amazingly real. An everlasting centerpiece, they never go bad, never rot, but their permanence is depressing. I should put something else there. I should get some new furniture. I should renovate my whole life.

"Your mom's in bed," Vicki says before she goes, "but I think she's still awake."

"Sorry you had so much trouble." I give her a good tip, hoping she'll come back if I need her.

My mother's room is dark, but I can hear her

breathing, the kind of breathing you do after you've cried a lot, with involuntary, irregular gasps of air.

"Mom? Are you okay?"

"Story," she says.

"You want a story?" She doesn't answer, but turns over and grabs my hand. Hers is cold and bony. Even in the dark, just touching her, I feel her fragility. She's losing weight. I know it's not my fault that she's old and sick, but the demons of illogic do their black magic, convince me that if I'd been a better daughter, this wouldn't be happening. During all those years after my father died and she lived in Columbia alone, I'd visited only once a month or so, for lunch before I had a meeting, or after a deposition. "Why don't you spend the night?" she'd ask. "We could go to the club."

I hated her downtown club, where all the waiters were black and all the members were white, and it irritated me that she spent so much of her paltry income on the membership fee. She knew I couldn't stand the place but never failed to make me feel guilty about not helping her "use up the monthly minimum."

"Besides," she'd say, "it wouldn't kill you to mingle with some nice people."

I tried not to fight with her but once when she was being particularly insistent I yelled, "You're always complaining about money. You hardly ever go to the club. You just want to say you're a member. Do what you want, but don't ask me to join you in your silliness." She *was* silly, and stuck in her ways, but I was cruel. I was angry because I wanted a mother who could understand me, who could love me for who I was.

Now as I hold her hand in the darkness of her bedroom, I remind myself that acceptance is a two-way street. She is who she is, or was.

I turn on the bedside lamp. "*Wind in the Willows* or *Travels with Charley*?"

"You were gone," she says, sitting up on her pillow.

"I had to interview a witness."

"Witness?"

"Remember I told you about the dog case? It's gotten kind of complicated." But she doesn't remember. Even if she could comprehend what's happened, she wouldn't understand how conflicted I feel about Joe. She's always adored him. "You're such a lucky girl," she'd said when we announced our engagement. Which meant— though she didn't say it then—that she couldn't believe someone as wonderful as Joe would fall in love with someone like me.

So of course she was horrified when I left him. *Are you out of your mind? Do you think you'll ever find another man like him?* Not once in those awful, lonely months after our separation did she say anything insightful or even comforting.

She assumed it was all my fault, and maybe it was. If I was a bad daughter, I was an even worse wife.

"So, do you want *Wind in the Willows* or *Charley*, Mom?"

"*Charley*."

"Okay." I find the place I marked, but it doesn't matter. She can't remember the story. She just likes the sound of my voice.

Charley likes to get up early, and he likes me to get up early too. And why shouldn't he? Right after his breakfast he goes back to sleep. Over the years he has developed a number of innocent-appearing ways to get me up.

She lets me read for a while, then asks, "Who's Charley?"

"He's Steinbeck's poodle. They go on a cross-country trip together." I continue:

He can shake himself and his collar loud enough to wake the dead. If that doesn't work he gets a sneezing fit. But perhaps his most irritating method is to sit quietly beside the bed and stare into my face with a sweet and forgiving look on his face; I come out of a deep sleep with the feeling of being looked at.

I think I hear her breathing slow, begin to settle into sleep, but then she stirs. "Charley and John, are they brothers?"

I close the book, turn off the light. "I'll tell you a true story. It's about the dog I represent. His name is Sherman. Remember, you met him that day at the beach. I'm trying to figure out whether he should live with the wife or the husband. I interviewed the vet today. He says—"

"Ask him," my mother mumbles.

"I did ask him, but he really doesn't have a strong opinion."

"The dog."

"Mom, the dog can't talk."

"But dogs can . . . tell you things."

I won't contradict her. "Okay, I'll try to be a better listener. I'm going to let you go to sleep now. Sleep tight."

When I lean over to kiss her on the cheek, she's already snoring.

Hours later, when I finally fall asleep myself, I dream that I've lost Sherman again and that I'm running up and down the beach screaming for him. When I find him, he looks at me with those intense black eyes, as if he's trying to tell me something. He jumps up, his paws on my knees. What is it he's trying to say?

Territorial

Monday morning I have a trial: short marriage, no children, no complicated legal issues, the kind of case that should have settled long ago but for the *real* issues—the emotional ones.

"I guess you won't see me for the rest of the day," I tell Gina before I leave the office. I look forward to the trial. The case has dragged on longer than it should have and my client, the husband, is blaming me, though I've done everything I can to move it along.

"They'll settle," Gina says.

"I doubt it."

But she's right. I've just finished cross-examining the wife when she asks for a break, and not long after that her lawyer approaches me with an offer that's almost identical to the one his client turned down a month ago. Though I'd like to believe my withering cross-examination has unnerved her, it's much more likely she just wanted to take the stand and tell the judge what an SOB her husband is, and now that she's gotten that over with, she's ready to be reasonable. I talk to my client. He's fuming. "She's cost me a couple thousand dollars more in attorney's fees, right?" But after a few more back-and-forths we reach an agreement and put it on the record.

I call Gina before I leave the courthouse. "We settled. I'm going to run by the post office, be back there in half an hour or so. Any crises?"

"Everything's under control. Mrs. Hart called, said she's dropping something off for you to look at. And Betty has something for you."

Betty, Judge Baynard's secretary, hands me an envelope. "It's the final order in that Anderson adoption," she says. "You okay?"

"Fine, just tired."

"You seem . . . I don't know . . . stressed."

"No more than usual."

"That's not what Gina says." Betty and Gina are old friends. They talk all the time. "She's worried about you, says you've been acting . . . She thought it might be about your mother, so I hope you don't mind that I told her about the other stuff that's going on."

"Other stuff?"

"Yeah. You know, between my judge and you."

I look her in the eye. "There is nothing going on between your judge and me." This comes out sharper than I mean it to. *"Nothing."*

I skip lunch, grab some crackers from the courthouse snack bar and stomp back to the office ready to explode at Gina, but Mrs. Hart is in my waiting room with Sherman, who sits politely at her feet.

"I just dropped by to bring these photo albums for you to look through," says Mrs. Hart, "but if you've got a moment—"

"Maybe I could watch Sherman while you talk," offers Gina.

Mrs. Hart frowns: "He doesn't really like . . . strangers."

"Oh, we'll be fine," says Gina. "I love dogs."

"Well, I suppose . . . but please let me know if he seems at all upset." She lets Sherman off his leash. "Stay, Sherman. Show this nice lady what a gentleman you are."

"Hold my calls, please," I tell Gina. Sherman sniffs her shoes and investigates the trash can, but concludes that it holds nothing of interest and settles down beside her desk.

I lead Mrs. Hart back to my office.

"I'm glad you can work me in," she says as she hands me a shopping bag that must weigh twenty pounds. It's stuffed with photo albums. "I've documented Sherman's life from the time we got him to the present. I think you'll find these very helpful."

"Thanks for bringing them."

"I'm sure you'll see how close our bond is," she says. "If Sherman could talk, he'd tell you."

And then I remember what my mother said the other night: *Dogs can tell you things.*

"Mrs. Hart, would you mind if I spend a little time with Sherman?"

"Of course not. I'll go get him."

"No, I mean . . . I'd like to spend some time with him, just the two of us. I promise I won't lose him again."

She looks nervous. I can't blame her. "I suppose it would be all right, but you must promise me you'll keep him on the leash. I couldn't bear it if something happened to him."

"I promise. Maybe you could do some shopping? Or there's that nice coffee shop down the street. I'll be back in an hour."

MEMO TO FILE:
HART V. HART

Walked Sherman from my office down Church Street to the Battery. He seems relaxed with me, though initially reluctant to leave Mrs. H. Does he sense her nervousness? Is this a problem? Long-term negative effect?

He's perhaps too friendly when meeting other dogs. (Vet said this was schnauzer personality.) Has no fear of bigger dogs. This almost gets him in trouble with a Great Dane. Maybe Mrs. Hart is wise to insist that he stay on a leash.

He pees a lot: tree trunks, lamp posts. Does this indicate some problem or is just territorial? (Ask vet.) Also tries to eat other dogs' poop. Unhealthy? (Ask vet.)

What I leave out of the memo is this:

It's slowgoing down to the Battery. He stops to sniff everything: lamp posts, parking meter poles, tree trunks. He seems totally absorbed in sniffing. We're within a couple of blocks of the Harts' downtown residence and several times he lifts his head, surveys the scene as if searching for his master, then he looks back at me and cocks his head in what seems like a question: *Where is he?*

And this: When the Great Dane growls at Sherman, I'm much more alarmed than Sherman is. I pull him back, pick him up, comfort him— though maybe he's the one doing the comforting. I like sitting on the bench with Sherman in my lap. I like running my fingers through his wiry outer coat to the soft fur underneath. He seems to like this, too, and likes it even more when I scratch him under his ears. I can feel his whole body relax. I'm not really doing anything, just serving as a cushion, but I feel useful, as if I have discovered a whole new purpose in life.

And my conversation with Sherman stays out of the memo, too. Okay, it isn't really a conversation, because he doesn't talk back, but he's an attentive listener.

I wish I could let you run around free, but I promised her I wouldn't let you off the leash. I wish you could tell me who you'd rather live with. I know, it's hard. You don't want to hurt their feelings, do you?

You like Dr. Borden, don't you? So do I. He seems wise, sweet. Maybe a little sad. What do you think that's all about? And he's sexy—but I guess I shouldn't be talking to you about that.

Anyway, we should be heading back to the office. She'll be worrying about you.

Another thing I leave out of the memo: On the way back to the office Sherman rolls in a pile of dog poop. He revels in it. How he manages to do this while I've got him on the leash, I don't know, but I'm realizing there's a lot I don't know. Before I can pull him away he's covered in the stuff. The leash gets a good dose, too. "Stop!" I yell, and yank hard. He turns his head and looks at me as if to say, *What's the problem? This is the best thing that's happened to me all day!*

I can't take him back looking like this. As we walk north on Meeting Street I see some painters working on the Calhoun Mansion. They have buckets and a hose.

"Mind if I rinse off my dog?" I ask them. They're delighted at the diversion, even if it's a slightly nasty one, and they help me with Sherman. We all get wet. I have to walk the dog around the block a couple of times before he stops dripping, and as we're walking I notice something: having an adorable dog trotting in front of me makes me a lot more noticeable. I'm suddenly very attractive. I'm the woman behind the adorable miniature schnauzer. Every half block or so someone stops me to ask his name, his breed. I'm content just to be along for the ride.

Mrs. Hart is pacing the sidewalk outside my office building. "I'm sorry," I say, "we were having such a nice time together."

She eyes me suspiciously. "I was worried," she says. "Come here, darling!" She bends down toward Sherman. "Mama missed you!" And then: "Why, he's *wet!*"

"We passed by some sprinklers."

Why do I feel a little disappointed when he wags his tail and barks that sharp little bark that I know means he's happy to see her?

Upstairs I confront Gina. "I'd appreciate it if you wouldn't talk to Betty about my personal life."

"What do you want me to do, hang up on her?" Gina's voice has that high-pitched, I-know-I've-screwed-up whine.

"I want you to tell her it's not appropriate to gossip about your boss."

"She was just trying to be helpful, sharing some information."

"Because you told her I hadn't been acting like myself, right?" My own voice has that high-pitched, I'm-really-pissed-off screech.

"I don't remember saying that."

"Did you say anything *like* that, maybe?"

"I just mentioned that you'd been a little . . . Is it really such a big deal?"

She's got me now. If I say *Yes, it's a big deal,* this will get back to Betty, then, who knows, maybe back to Joe. "No, it's not a big deal, but I don't want it to happen again, okay?"

"Okay." Gina hands me a stack of phone messages and I pretend to look through them, but the truce doesn't last long.

"While we're on the subject," she says, "if you'd just give me some information now and then, I wouldn't have to hear it from other sources."

"Like, what kind of information?"

"Like Judge Joe leaving his wife, telling her he's in love with you, that he's never for one minute been *out* of love with you."

"I didn't know anything until Ellen—"

"Oh, come on. I thought we were friends."

"We are, but we won't be if you don't stop." I go back to my office, fuming.

An hour later she knocks on the door. "I've just about finished with the draft of Dr. Borden's affidavit and the motion to bifurcate."

"I'll look it over later."

"But you'll need it tonight, won't you?"

"What?"

"He called while you were out with the dog, said something about coming by after his clinic closes so he could look over the affidavit."

"I can't stay late tonight. It's not fair to Delores, and it's too late to call Vicki again. Tell him we'll fax it."

"But I thought you said you wanted to file it ASAP . . . That's what I told him, which is why he offered to come by after work."

"Tell him you'll fax it, he can look it over, and if it's okay, you can take it to him tomorrow for his signature."

Gina perks up. "He sounded nice. Married?"

"I think so." I lie. It's instinctive, territorial.

"Too bad. Listen, Sally . . ."

"What?"

"I'm really sorry . . . about the thing with Betty."

"Apology accepted. And I'm sorry for yelling." I go back to my work. On any other afternoon the stacks of files might feel overwhelming, but today they're reassuring, familiar and safe, the kind of problems I know how to solve. I attack them one by one, making notes, drafting memos, formulating strategies.

At solving other people's problems, I'm a master.

It's Complicated

I get home a little early. The condo is quiet: no Delores, no Mom. I panic until I remember they drove out to Middleton Plantation for the afternoon.

This morning I'd reminded my mother about the outing. "You always like the plantation, don't you, Mom?"

She shook her head. "We lost the plantation."

"That's right, Mom, we don't have the plantation anymore." I'm talking nonsense, but only part of it has to do with her Alzheimer's. She's always believed in the myth of her family's lost plantation, kept it alive as a kind of antidote to her middle-class existence. As a child I believed in it myself—the thousand acres of fertile South Carolina land, the big house, the fine furniture, the family portraits painted by famous artists, all stolen by marauding Yankees—until one day an older cousin revealed the truth: that the place was just a small farm and the ancestors who'd owned it weren't rich at all, just hard-scrabble folks who'd lost the land during the Depression.

I used to argue with my mother about "the plantation," scold her about the danger of such myths, make speeches about how much better it is to be self-made and self-sufficient than to depend on inherited wealth. She never listened. "You come from a *very* prominent family, Sally. Don't forget it."

But I don't argue with her anymore. Delores taught me this. "She lives in her own world now. No use trying to pull her into yours. You just upset her. If she thinks she's the Queen of England, don't cross her, just say, 'It must be nice, having all those castles and jewels.'"

"But isn't it wrong," I said, "to lie to her like that?"

"You're just going along, to get along," said Delores.

I've read a dozen books about Alzheimer's, talked to three specialists, and yet I don't think I have half the wisdom Delores has about my mother. She knows there'll be good days and bad days and even worse days. She knows that no matter how hard she tries to be a good caregiver, there'll be bad days, but she doesn't punish herself with guilt. After the disastrous afternoon at the beach she apologized for dozing off, as she should have, but I know she does her best, and her best is much better than mine would be if I stayed with my mother eight hours a day, five days a week. I often wonder how Delores manages to maintain her generally good mood, her patience, and her sense of humor.

But this afternoon when they get home Delores' smile isn't convincing. There are circles under her eyes. "Did everything go okay at Middleton?" I ask.

"Yes, ma'am. She sure likes that place."

"But maybe it's too much, taking her all the way out there. You look exhausted."

"No, I like seeing her have such a good time." Delores gathers her things and says good-bye but then lingers at the door, as if she's too tired to turn the knob.

"What's wrong?" I ask.

"We need to talk," she says, turning around.

We sit across from each other in the living room. Delores smoothes her wrinkled slacks, strokes her thighs as if trying to calm herself. It's then that I notice the ring on her left hand. A small diamond.

"It's beautiful, Delores."

She nods. "That's what I need to talk to you about." She turns to my mother, who's beside her on the sofa, yawning. "You sleepy, honey? Ready for bed?"

"But she hasn't had any dinner."

"We had a little snack on the way back. Come on, Miz Margaret, let's get into your nightgown."

How many times, I think, has Delores sermonized on the pitfalls of marriage? But when she comes back I do my best to sound enthusiastic. "Congratulations! When's the big day?"

"As soon as we can," she says, but she looks

grim. "Charlie's sick." She bursts into tears. "Cancer. It's bad."

"When did all this . . . I had no idea." But I know she doesn't like to bother me with her problems, and I've been so distracted lately.

"He had some bleeding. They put him in the hospital. When they opened him up, it was all over the place."

"You should have told me. I'm so sorry."

"I need to be with him."

"Of course you do."

She smiles, relieved. "Charlie wants to make us legal, so we're getting married. And he wanted to do it right, with this engagement ring and all. I don't want to argue with him, not now."

"No, I can understand that."

"So I'll be leaving in a month or so, if that's all right. I just hate to leave Miz Margaret. And you, too. Y'all like family to me."

I feel the panic sear through me like an electric shock. "Don't worry about us. You have enough on your hands."

"I can ask around to see if I can help you find somebody else," she offers. "Vicki's got her day job, but I know some others. And maybe it's time to think about putting her someplace where she can get the kind of care she needs."

"What?"

"She's going to take this hard, me leaving. And you might have to move her soon anyway."

"Why would I have to move her?"

"Pretty soon she's going to need a lot more help, not just in the daytime, but maybe at night, too."

"I'm here at night."

"But you can't be up and down with her all the time, helping her get to the bathroom. You need your sleep."

"I promised her I wouldn't put her in a nursing home."

"That was a long time ago. You've already done way more than most children do. I know what she'd tell you if she were in her right mind."

"Nobody can know that."

Delores straightens her spine, rises. "I do. She told me when I first came on the job. 'Delores,' she said, 'I know my girl. She's stubborn as an ox. When the time comes,' your mama said, 'You tell her this, you tell her I want her to have a life. Her *own* life.'"

"That doesn't sound like Mom."

"Maybe you don't know her like you think you do."

I open the refrigerator, nose around for leftovers, spot a bottle of wine that's been around for months, and pour myself a glass. "You should drink more," Joe used to say. "A glass of wine every now and then won't kill you. You might even like me better!" I turn the radio on, NPR, but the news is all bleak, so I switch to an oldies station and sing along with Carole King.

I barely hear the doorbell when it rings. Through the peephole, Dr. Borden's face looms large.

"Hi," he says, as if he visits me at home every day.

I open the door. "Hi," I say. And then I see the dog beside him. A beagle.

"I went by your office to look over the affidavit, but you'd already left."

"I asked Gina to fax it to you. I'm sorry you had to come all the way—"

"My fax machine hasn't worked in months. She said she didn't mind staying until I could pick it up."

Yes, I think, I'm sure Gina didn't mind staying.

"I'd like to make a few changes," he says, "so she gave me your address. Don't be upset with her. She's quite protective of you! I had to do a lot of convincing. Hope I'm not interrupting your dinner or anything."

"No. I was just having a glass of wine." Actually I'm already on my second. "Would you like one?"

"Sure. I can't stay long, but I do have an ulterior motive." He looks down at the beagle. "Hope you don't mind that I brought Carmen. This is the dog I was telling you about, the abandoned one. Shake hands with Ms. Baynard, Carmen." The beagle sits, lifts her paw. "I almost brought

Sherman along, too, but I thought that might be a little much."

"Why do you have Sherman?"

"Maryann Hart dropped him off at the clinic yesterday for a booster, asked us to board him overnight. Must be out of town, I guess. I was surprised she didn't just let Rusty keep him."

"Happens all the time in custody cases," I say. "Mom, who has custody, hires a babysitter to stay with the kids rather than let Dad have a few extra hours. Sit down, I'll get your wine." I leave him in the living room, and for the first time ever I'm embarrassed by the mismatched furniture: some of my mother's, some of my own, a mix that comes across as more haphazard than eclectic.

"Mind if I let Carmen off the leash?" He doesn't wait for me to answer. The beagle follows me into the kitchen. She sits beside the kitchen table while I pour some wine for the vet and another glass for me. *Keep it businesslike,* I tell myself, though I'm not feeling at all businesslike.

"Funny," Dr. Borden says when I return, "I didn't imagine you in a place like this. It's very nice, but . . . I pictured you in a little house at the beach. Folly Beach, maybe."

That he would picture me anywhere at all is nice. "It's near my office. No yard, no maintenance. And there's a great view from the deck. My mother likes it."

"Where is she, by the way?"

"Sleeping. I think she's down for the night. If it's not too chilly, we can sit on the deck. Carmen, you want to see the harbor?"

I take a dish towel to wipe off the chairs. The sun is setting, and I squint to read his notes on the affidavit. "You've scratched out the sentence about how the shared custody schedule isn't good for Sherman," I say.

"Because he seems to be doing okay," says Dr. Borden. The last of the sunlight accentuates the little vertical wrinkle between his eyes, his strong nose, the way his hair curls in the damp air.

"But don't you think that's just because it's only been a couple of weeks since the temporary order? You told me you wouldn't recommend this back-and-forth arrangement as a permanent thing, right?"

"I wouldn't."

He looks out across the darkening water, mulls this. "Maybe I could say, 'While I haven't observed any harm to Sherman as the result of the court's temporary order, I would hesitate to recommend a shared schedule on a permanent basis.' How's that sound?"

"If you're going to insist that the temporary order isn't hurting Sherman, you're taking away my best argument for hurrying up the trial. I was planning to use your affidavit to support the motion to bifurcate." I'm a little drunk, but I hear myself sounding way too professional.

"What about this? 'Although Sherman is healthy and suffering no apparent distress at the present time, I believe it would be in his best interests
to settle the issue of his custody as soon as reasonably possible.'"

"That should work," I say.

"So, what do you think about Carmen?" The beagle points her nose to the sky, sampling the salt air, the smell of the harbor, then, as if on cue, nuzzles her head against my leg.

"She's sweet, but my life is way too complicated right now. I won't bore you with the details. I just can't make any more commitments." This is coming out all wrong.

"Okay," he says. He scribbles on the affidavit as if he's in a huge hurry, then hands me the pen, his fingers brushing mine. "Come on, Carmen. Let's let Ms. Baynard have a peaceful evening." Before he leaves he puts his empty glass on the kitchen counter. "Thanks for the wine."

At the door Carmen looks up at me, disappointed. *I like you. He likes you. But you really blew it, lady.*

A Real Bitch

W ell," says Gina the next morning, "how did it go?"

"None of your business."

"You're mad that I gave him your address."

"No."

"You sound mad."

"I'm not mad," I say, not very convincingly. "I'm just not going to give you a report."

"He was really insistent. The guy has the hots for you!"

"What makes you think that?"

"Maybe that he drives all the way into town to pick up an affidavit, then insists that he wants to talk to you in person?"

"He was trying to convince me to adopt a dog."

"Yeah, right," says Gina. "She's a sweetheart, but that's not what he wanted. He brought her in here, but he didn't ask *me* if I wanted her. He was in too much of a hurry."

"You should have called me to let me know he was coming."

"He doesn't seem like the dangerous type," she says. "Not much of a womanizer."

"What's your evidence for that?"

"He wouldn't even flirt."

"Oh, so you tried, huh?"

"Not too hard, but like I say, I could tell he was really determined to see you, so I didn't give it my total effort." She smiles that mock-wicked smile of hers. "So, you're not going to tell me how it went?"

I ignore the question, start down the hall toward my office. Gina calls after me: "Mrs. Carter called to say she's running a few minutes late. You'll need to leave by eleven so you can drive out to Sullivan's Island for the interview with that girl who lives next to Mrs. Hart. Mindy something. And in case you don't get back to the office afterward, remember about the motion hearing first thing in the morning—about the vet's fees."

"If I only take up half an hour of your time," says Natalie Carter, who's come in for an initial consultation, "will you cut the fee?" She's agitated about the $300 charge for the hour and a half conference, during which I get the basic facts of the case, assess the situation, and give her my recommendations. Meanwhile, I can't help noticing her baby blue purse and matching heels, which together probably cost at least twice that.

"I'm sure it will take at least an hour and a half, maybe longer, for me to get the basic information I need to evaluate your case."

"What do you mean, 'evaluate'? We have

plenty of assets, if that's what you're interested in."

I try not to show my irritation. "As I'm sure my secretary told you when she made the appointment, this first meeting is for me to gather some facts about your situation, then tell you what I think you ought to do. And of course you'll want to ask questions. Then we'll both need to decide if we're a good fit. You may decide you don't want to hire me." I don't say: *And I may decide I don't want to represent you.*

"I've tried to find a lawyer in Beaufort, but no one will take the case because of who my husband is." She looks out the window to the garden across the alley. "They should do something about that yard. Some people just don't take any responsibility for their property."

I've always liked the overgrown garden with its curving brick paths, the huge old magnolia, the sprawling azaleas beneath it. I go there in my daydreams sometimes when I should be working on a brief. For a moment I'm that young woman who sits there in the morning sun reading the newspaper, or who waters the flowers or who plays with her two little girls who come in the afternoon.

Mrs. Carter fingers her gold bracelet. "You know who my husband is, right?"

"Yes."

Derwood Carter is a circuit judge from

Beaufort, an hour and a half away, who some-times holds court in Charleston. It's been my misfortune to appear before him several times. He's a high-born snob who hates his weeks in criminal court, where he presides over cases involving, as I've heard him say, "the welfare class." All the public defenders do their best to avoid him; he usually opts for the maximum sentence. He's mean, but smart, and he conducts his trials so that there isn't much error to exploit on appeal.

"Derwood says you're a real bitch," Mrs. Carter smiles. "That's why I thought I should hire you."

"I don't think he likes female lawyers."

"He only likes women who are subservient, and preferably those who perform disgusting sexual . . . I'm sure you know about his relationship with his court reporter—"

This is an enticing morsel, but I can't get side-tracked. "We'll come back to that, okay? I need to get some basic information first. How long have you been married?"

Most lawyers let their secretaries or paralegals handle this initial fact-gathering, but I like to do it myself. Every marriage is a story, and it's not just the narrative that matters but the voice of the narrator. Is she angry? Sad? Both? Is she arrogant, vengeful? Are there questions she hesitates to answer?

After half an hour Mrs. Carter asks for a break. 'I haven't smoked in years, but now I . . . I'll just be a minute." She takes the elevator downstairs and paces back and forth on the sidewalk in front of my office, not really smoking, just holding the lit cigarette. I sneak in a call to Tony Borden. "I'm sorry," says his receptionist. "He's busy with an emergency."

"Please tell him I called. Nothing urgent." I give her my cell phone number and watch Mrs. Carter drop the cigarette to the pavement and stamp it out with more force than necessary. She looks up and down Broad Street as if she thinks she's being followed. She's a wreck—so thin she seems breakable—and who wouldn't be, married to Derwood Carter for twenty-five years? That's a worse sentence than any he's ever doled out.

I'll take her case. She'll probably drive me crazy. And it will drive her husband crazy that she's hired "that bitch Sarah Baynard." I look forward to his deposition, when I'll look across the conference table and ask him about his relationship with his court reporter.

It's Reality

As I cross the bridge to Sullivan's Island, I'm rehearsing my apology to Tony Borden. *I'm sorry, I didn't mean to be rude about the beagle. It's just that . . . things are so complicated right now . . . I hope you'll be patient.* Does that help any? I doubt it, but it doesn't matter, because he doesn't call.

"Oh, I forgot you were coming," says Mindy Greene. She's cracked the door open just wide enough to let me see half her face and a glimpse of her black bra and panties. "I'm kinda, not . . . Can you hold on a minute?" I wait on the front porch, look across the driveway to the Harts' house. Mrs. Hart's Mercedes is in the carport.

When Mindy comes back to let me in she's wearing a light blue College of Charleston sweatshirt and black tights that hug her ample bottom and stocky legs. "Sorry, like I said, I forgot. You want a beer or something?"

"No thanks."

"Might have one myself." She's off to the kitchen. "Go ahead and sit down if you want to," she yells. I hear the can pop. The house is one of the old Sullivan's Island houses, like the Harts', but it hasn't been redecorated in quite a while: it's like a museum to the nineteen fifties.

"You live here by yourself?" I ask.

"Yep. My grandmother left it to me in her will. I think she did it mostly to piss off my parents. She and my dad don't get along."

"So, how long have you lived here?"

"Four . . . five years."

"And you're a student at the College of Charleston?"

She laughs, takes a swig of her Coors. "Yeah, barely."

"What year?" I'm taking notes.

"Whadya mean?"

"Freshman, sophomore?"

"Oh. Well, it's kinda, you know, hard to tell . . . The thing is, I didn't really want to go to college in the first place, but my grandmother put this thing in her will that I hafta graduate or else the house goes to some charity."

"Are you going full-time, or do you work?"

"I take a couple of courses a semester, but I've flunked a few, so . . . No, I don't work. She left me some dough. Sure I can't get you something to drink? You look like you could use one!"

What does she see? A middle-aged lawyer in her little brown suit and sensible pumps, dark circles under the eyes. "I don't drink while I'm working. You understand why I'm here?"

"Yeah. It's ridiculous."

"Mrs. Hart—"

"She's completely nuts."

"Mrs. Hart has alleged that you, uh, had sexual relations with her husband, but the other lawyers will be dealing with that. I'm really more interested in—"

"You know what? The old dude can't even get it up anymore."

"How do you know that?"

"'Cause he told me. We're kinda like, you know, confidentials."

"Confidants?"

"Yeah, that's it."

"So you feel you know Mr. Hart pretty well?"

"Better than his own wife does, I guess you could say."

"And how would you describe him?"

"Sad. He's just a sad old man."

I remember the detective's affidavit: *Elderly male subject and young woman later identified as Mindy Greene observed embracing and kissing on sofa in Hart beach residence. Some minutes later they share what appears to be a marijuana cigarette.*

"Has he ever kissed you?"

"Sure. I know what you're talking about. And that night wasn't the first time, either. But it wasn't like . . . I mean, it wasn't a passion thing."

"What was it, then?"

"Just an old-man kiss. I didn't mind. He's kinda like a grandfather or something. He doesn't mean anything by it."

"So there was no other . . . no sex."

She laughs so hard she sends beer spray toward me. "I told you, he can't get it up. And even if he could, he wouldn't. He's a gentleman."

"What about the marijuana?"

"Yeah, I guess I gotta admit to that. He just wanted to try it."

"So, you brought it over?"

"Right. He was feeling depressed, and I said, hey, you know man, when I need a little lift, I have a toke. So he tried it. But he didn't like it. You need to write all this down?"

"I'm just trying to understand—"

"Good luck with that. Here's what it looks like to me: two old married people get bored with each other. Nothing unusual, right? Then they have some kind of dumb argument and she tells him she doesn't want to live with him anymore, sends him out here to the beach house. But then the old man doesn't say, 'Let's get back together,' because, you know what, he's not miserable without her, in fact he realizes he was miserable *with* her, but he'd been kinda sup—oh, I forgot the word, you know, for when you feel something but you can't admit it to yourself . . ."

"Suppressing?"

"Yeah. He's been suppressing how bad he's felt for so many years and now it's just a relief to be living apart. So he doesn't say, 'Hey, let's get back together.' He just lets things ride. He's okay living out here in the beach house. Matter of fact, he'd rather be out here than in that fancy place down-town. And this drives her crazy, 'cause she's a control freak, and things aren't going according to plan. So she gets herself a fancy downtown lawyer and they hire a dick to watch him out here, and what do you know, even though the dick can hardly hold his damn video camera he gets lucky one night and shoots these pictures of me and Mr. Hart doing stuff, I mean not really *anything,* like I told you, but I guess to a judge it looks—have you seen it? The video, I mean?"

"No, but I've read the detective's report. Where was the dog during all this?"

"He was sleeping. Like I say, it wasn't all that exciting."

"What I really want to focus on is Sherman, how the Harts relate to him. Have you had the opportunity to observe that?"

"Yeah, more with him than her. When they were together she was always kinda standoffish. And now since she thinks—I mean, since she thinks there's all this adultery stuff, she won't even speak to me."

"But let's go back to before they separated. How much time did they spend out here at the beach?"

"They'd come out a lot in the winter. Not so much in the summer. And sometimes he'd come by himself for a few days and bring the dog.

170

That's how we got to know each other. He knew my grandmother, and I guess she must have asked him to look out for me."

"How did he look out for you?"

"If he was ordering in a pizza or something he'd knock on my door, 'cause he knew I was all by myself, and ask me if I'd like some. Or if there was a storm and the power went off he'd check to see if I was okay. Things like that. And then we got to be friends, and he'd come out here by himself more, and he'd invite me over to watch a movie or talk."

"What did you talk about?"

"I don't know. Things. He was just lonely."

"But you said he seemed happier without her."

"I wouldn't say happier. He was just relieved not to have to deal with her. But he's not a happy camper. He's got this real gloomy view of things, like the whole world is going to hell. Says nobody plays by the rules anymore, nobody's honest, the whole country's crazy, the government's corrupt. Yada, yada, yada. But anyway, he's interesting to talk to. Really smart. Full of opinions. And he always asks me stuff about my life, like he's really interested. But not like, you know, in a creepy sort of way. And then he started helping me with my school stuff. I had this Econ 101 that was a real bitch of a course."

"So he was tutoring you?"

"Yeah, I guess you could say that. He used to

be a banker, so he understands all that stuff. He was real patient with me. I'm not, you know, that great when it comes to math and graphs and stuff."

"What's your major?"

"Business. One of these days I want to open my own nail parlor. We need another one out here on the beach."

"So, how much time would you say you spent with Mr. Hart before his wife filed the divorce case?"

"Not that much, but I guess it was enough to piss her off. Once, before she hired the detective, she left a note in my mailbox, like, you know, *My husband is not emotionally well,* or something like that, and said it wouldn't be a good idea to spend too much time with him, 'cause he might take it the wrong way. It was really weird."

"Do you have the note?"

"Nah. I threw it away. She's the nut in the family, if you ask me."

"Did you tell Mr. Hart about it?"

"Sure. He told me to forget it. I was in the middle of studying for the final in the econ course, and he wasn't going to let me down."

"And so, going back to the dog—when Mr. Hart spent time out here, would he bring Sherman?"

"Most of the time. Sherman likes the beach."

"And what were your observations about how Mr. Hart relates to the dog?"

"He relates great. I think he'd rather be with Sherman than anybody in the world." Mindy tips the beer can up, sticks her tongue out to collect the last drops. "This going to take a lot longer?"

"Do you have someplace to go?"

"No, but I don't want to miss my show."

"What show?"

"*Bride Diaries.* Comes on at six, but I guess I could TiVo it. You watch?"

"No."

"So cool. I love reality shows. This one's the best. They follow these girls who just got engaged, all the prewedding stuff. Shopping for the dress, planning the ceremony. Lots of stress, so naturally there's a lot of drama with the fiancé, sometimes with the crazy mothers. And sometimes they split up before the wedding. It's reality, so nobody knows what's going to happen until it happens. You should try it."

"I get enough reality at work."

"You can learn a lot about relationships. Why they get screwed up and all."

"When you figure that out, let me know."

Mindy laughs. "That's another thing about Mr. Hart. He can talk real honest about things like that. Feelings and all. When I'd get upset about my love life—or I should say *non*love life—he'd calm me down. Always made me feel better about myself. Like I'm not this fat dumb chick who'll never find a guy."

"And what about Mrs. Hart? How does she relate to Sherman?"

"Well, I haven't seen her that much alone with him."

"What about since she's been living out here?"

"Like I said, she won't even speak to me. Sometimes I see her when she takes Sherman out for a pee, but she pretends not to notice me."

"She has a maid?"

"Yeah. I think she comes once or twice a week."

"Have you ever seen the maid taking Sherman for a walk?"

"Yeah, once or twice, maybe. I try not to butt into the old lady's business, except that I can't help notice, like last night, I saw her coming in at about three in the morning. And that wasn't the first time. Every couple of weeks or so she goes out late at night. Who knows, maybe *she's* the one who's screwing around."

"Did she take Sherman?" I know where Sherman was last night. I'm just testing her.

"You'd have to ask *her* that. I just happened to be up, saw the car coming into the garage. I wasn't spying."

"Just one more question," I say, flipping to a

new page on my legal pad. "Have you ever observed either Mr. or Mrs. Hart doing anything which might harm Sherman, or put him in danger?"

"Oh, I know what you're getting at. The old lady used to be on his case all the time about not letting Sherman off the leash. I think he just does it—I mean, let the dog off the leash—to irritate her."

"But didn't he break his foot or something?"

"Yeah, and the old man felt really bad about that, even though it wasn't his fault. They were just crossing the street, and this jerk comes around the corner going about sixty miles an hour, way over the speed limit, and hits Sherman. It would have happened even if the dog had been on the leash. At least that's what Mr. Hart told me."

"What about Mrs. Hart. Have you ever seen her intoxicated?"

"She gets pretty happy on her wine, but I've never seen her falling-down drunk, if that's what you mean."

"And what about Mr. Hart?"

"He has some bourbon every now and then, but nothing over-the-top."

"I think I already know your answer to this, but if you had to choose between the two of them, which one would do a better job of taking care of Sherman?"

She surprises me. "To be fair, I just don't know. I know she takes good care of him, like she's his mama."

"How do you know that, if you don't see her with the dog that often."

"'Cause Mr. Hart told me. Before all this divorce stuff started up, he told me he thought his wife loved Sherman more than she loved him. He seemed kinda jealous. You know what?"

"What?"

"I think the dog is sorta like their child. It's pathetic. And they really know how to screw up a kid!"

"Oh, I think Sherman's doing okay."

"I'm not talking about the dog."

"What kid are you talking about, then?"

She looks genuinely dismayed. "Mr. Hart doesn't like me bringing it up. And it doesn't matter anyway, not to the case."

"Why don't you let me decide if it matters or not?"

"Look, I'm not going to say anything else about that." She sighs a dramatic sigh.

"I'll ask you about it at your deposition, so you might as well—"

"If you're going to be much longer, I can TiVo my show." She reaches for the remote.

"No, I'm finished. Thanks for your time."

"Hey, this deposition thing, what's that all about, anyway?" Mindy's deposition is scheduled sometime in the next couple of weeks. "A friend of mine said maybe I should get a lawyer."

"You could talk to one." I give her a few names.

"Thanks," she says. "Sure you wouldn't like a beer for the road?" I shake my head.

"Well, take it easy. Must be exciting, being a lawyer and all. But lots of stress, too, right? So, like Mr. Hart tells me, 'Give yourself a break,' okay?"

On the drive back to the office I can't get Mindy's voice out of my head. Maybe she's not so dumb after all. I turn on the radio, catch Bonnie Raitt in the middle of "Let's Give 'Em Something to Talk About," and then, as if summoned by the song, Tony Borden calls.

"Sorry I didn't get back to you earlier, had a real busy day." He sounds distant, distracted.

"I apologize for last night. I didn't mean to be so . . . discouraging."

"Don't worry, I'll manage. Maybe it will even be interesting."

"What?"

"The case," he says. "Maybe it'll be interesting, my first dog-custody trial."

"No, I meant I shouldn't have been so discouraging about the beagle."

He answers in that same disinterested tone: "You've got a lot going on in your life. I understand."

"Maybe things will be clearer after this case is over."

"Take all the time you want. Meanwhile I'll be looking for somebody who's not quite so busy."

When he hangs up, I feel like turning around, going back to Mindy Greene's house, maybe watching *Bride Diaries* with her, having a few beers, trying a little reality TV. Maybe, as she says, I could learn a little something about relationships.

The Devil in the Details

There's a force at work in the universe—or at least the mini-universe of my home and office—which seems to derive its pleasure from watching me cope with trouble. Some days its imagination is particularly active. For example, this morning before I even left the condo:

—My mother dropped her glasses down the disposal and then forgot about them, so that when I flipped the switch to grind a rotten tomato, there was a sound like a five-car pileup in my kitchen.

—In the middle of my shower, with my hair full of shampoo, I found myself without water, and only then remembered the notice stuck to the front door yesterday: WATER WILL BE SHUT OFF FOR REPAIR WORK, 8-10 A.M. WEDNESDAY. THANK YOU FOR YOUR PATIENCE.

—After I'd rinsed my hair with ice-cold water from the fridge, I looked through the closet for something not too dowdy to wear to court, something which might improve my spirits, but found only the familiar black and brown and gray suits, all appropriate but depressing, so I chose a green wool dress I hadn't worn in years, but the back zipper stuck halfway open. My mother, of course, was no help in this clothing emergency.

—Delores was late (her car wouldn't start), and after she helped me with the zipper she chose this time to let me know that she would definitely be leaving in three weeks and to ask me if I'd thought about putting "Miz Margaret in a home." I snapped at her, then apologized, but on the drive to work I cried, which made my mascara run, which made me feel ridiculous.

I cross-examined myself: *You wear mascara about once a decade. Why today? Does it have anything to do with the fact that Judge Baynard will be presiding in the dog case? So it's true, isn't it, Ms. Baynard, that you're enjoying his attention?*

At the office the devil continued to entertain himself at my expense.

"Rick Silber says he's having trouble with the interrogatories," says Gina.

"He just needs to draft some responses. We'll fine-tune them."

"I told him that. But he says he just can't face it, it's too painful."

"Oh, for God's sake, he's a psychologist!"

"He suggested it might be easier if I came to his house."

"Easier on whom?"

"I don't mind. I can go after work."

"It's just a ploy to get in your pants."

"Oh, I don't think so. He's not the type."

"He was 'the type' with his grad student, remember?"

"He sounded really pathetic on the phone."

"He's good at that."

"Don't be so cynical. By the way, Natalie Carter sent a retainer check and the signed retainer agreement, but the check was only half of what you quoted. And right after I opened the envelope her husband called, wanted to talk to you about the case. I guess she must have told him she hired you."

"I'm not going to talk to him directly. Call him back and ask him who's representing him."

"What do you want me to do with her check?"

"Deposit it, I guess. I'll deal with the rest later."

"Okay. And I almost forgot to tell you, Dr. Borden signed the revised affidavit."

"When?"

"I took it to him yesterday afternoon."

"You're being awfully accommodating, Gina."

"I live out that way, remember? He's adorable, but that clinic of his could use a woman's touch

. . . Maybe some nice tile instead of that ancient linoleum, and some new furniture."

"You better decide how you're going to spend your energy, Gina—tending to the psychologist who can't bear to answer interrogatories or the vet who needs a decorator."

"Geez, you don't have to get so pissy."

"It's been a bad morning." But I don't have time to go into detail because I'm late for court.

"One more thing before you go," she says. "I was looking through those photo albums Mrs. Hart brought in. Look at this." She points to a photo of Sherman curled up on a bed.

"He's cute. But we already knew that," I say.

"I'm not talking about Sherman. Look at that plaque on the wall behind him."

I have to squint to read the writing:

Anna B. Hart
Student Citizenship Award

"So?" I say, already halfway to the door.

"I can't read the whole date, but it looks like this Anna would be in her thirties. You told me they didn't have any children, and I checked the pleadings. Sure enough, look at Mrs. Hart's complaint. Here it is: *There are no children of the marriage.* And Mr. Hart doesn't say anything to the contrary in his answer."

"Could be a niece or something."

"People don't hang plaques like that for their nieces."

"Maybe it's just a mistake in the complaint."

"Then why wouldn't he correct it?"

"Because it doesn't really matter. They're fighting over Sherman, not a grown-up daughter."

Gina persists: "You've always told me that when people go to this much trouble to hide something, there's a reason. Here, as long as you're going to the courthouse, you might as well take the vet's affidavit and the motion to bifurcate."

He Deserves It

The family court waiting area is overflowing with men, mostly in their twenties and thirties, and though it's only ten in the morning, they look as if they've spent the night here. This is what the lawyers call "Deadbeat Dad Day," the Department of Social Services' once-a-month roundup of fathers who've failed to pay child support. These guys—and a sprinkling of women—will appear before a judge to offer their excuses:

—Why should I pay her anything? She don't spend the money on the kids; she spends it on herself.
—I had to make my car payment. If I lose my car, I lose my job.
—I got two other kids in California, and one in New York.

And so on. The excuses run from lame to pathetic, with an occasional one that might earn the defendant a reprieve: *Judge, I lost my job six months ago. Here's a list of the places I've looked for work.* I've been appointed on so many of these cases, they all blend together in my head. At least this morning I can walk past the crowd of miserable men without having to look anyone in the eye and see that panic when I say, "I'll do my best, but you're probably going to jail." Some of these guys look familiar. I move quickly so no one can grab me.

But it isn't a desperate delinquent dad who reaches out to touch my arm. It's the vet. "Good morning," he says, but not warmly. "Can we get this over with? I've got a clinic full of animals waiting. I don't appreciate having some thug knock on my door at eleven at night with a subpoena." He hands it to me.

"I didn't have anything to do with this. It's from Mrs. Hart's lawyer."

"Do I have to stay, then? Like I said, I've got a full load at the clinic." He's holding a file marked HART, SHERMAN.

"Yes, but it shouldn't take too long—fifteen minutes, half an hour at the most. And as long as you're here, we'll make sure your overdue bill gets paid."

He follows me into the courtroom where Henry Swinton is waiting with Mrs. Hart. She nods my way. Just at the stroke of ten Michelle Marvel rushes in, her five-inch heels digging into the carpet, her mass of red hair even more dramatic than usual—did the wind do this, or is it some new product?—with Mr. Hart galumphing behind her, breathless.

"All rise!" announces the court reporter. "*Hart v.*

Hart, Defendant's motion to require plaintiff to pay veterinarian's fees."

Joe Baynard is still zipping up his robe as he takes the bench. "Take your seats, please," he says. But I don't. He notices. "Ms. Baynard, you have something to say before we proceed with Mr. Hart's motion?"

"Yes, your honor. This is Dr. Tony Borden, the veterinarian. He is here because Mr. Swinton had him served—at eleven last night—with a subpoena." I hand the paper to my ex-husband, at which point Henry Swinton jumps to his feet. I hear him inhale in preparation for a speech, but I cut him off. "There is no excuse for this late notice. While I don't represent Dr. Borden, I would ask the court to order that Mr. Swinton—not his client—pay Dr. Borden's fees as an expert witness, plus an additional amount in the court's discretion, considering the late notice and the fact that Dr. Borden is missing an entire morning of appointments." Tony Borden's sitting as far back in the courtroom as he can get.

Henry Swinton puffs up. "We apologize, your honor. My secretary is new, and this was her mistake." His righteousness is almost convincing.

Michelle Marvel jumps up. "We're distressed that Dr. Borden has had his schedule interrupted without proper notice, your honor, but as long as he's here, we hope he can testify as to matters pertinent to the welfare of the dog."

Henry Swinton slaps his pen on the table. "Judge, this hearing has nothing to do with the welfare of the dog. We are here on my client's motion for an order clarifying the temporary order by requiring Mr. Hart to pay the vet's fees, because, as your honor will soon be convinced, Mr. Hart's negligence has inflated those fees."

Michelle Marvel: "Your honor, the temporary order requires Mr. Hart to pay his wife a very generous monthly alimony payment, which he has been paying in a timely fashion. Your honor set the alimony amount based on Mrs. Hart's sworn financial declaration, which listed monthly expenses—including her estimate of the veterinary costs—and it is therefore her responsibility to pay those expenses, at least until the trial."

If this were any other case in family court, Joe would listen to the lawyers for a total of maybe five minutes, then announce his decision. But this is "the dog case," as I've heard it referred to at the coffee shop, and the usual rules don't seem to apply. So I'm not really surprised when Joe says, "I'll hear the plaintiff's motion regarding the payment of Dr. Borden's veterinary fees, and then if there are matters pertaining to the welfare of the dog, I'll be happy to consider those as well. Ms. Baynard, as guardian for the animal, I'm sure you're interested in his welfare." He doesn't wait for me to object, because he knows I can't. "Dr. Borden, I thank you for your patience. You may proceed with your motion, Mr. Swinton."

My ex-husband leans back in his fake-leather chair, then forward, then back again, bobbing lazily, fiddling with the zipper on his black robe, leaning back again so far I think he might disappear altogether, then rising and looking back at me, smiling, as if he has all the time in the world. I should be angry with him, but I like the smile. I've missed it.

Henry Swinton calls Tony Borden to the stand. "Dr. Borden, you have provided veterinary services for the dog for the past five years, is that correct?"

"Four and a half, actually."

"You brought your billing file with you, as well as your records of the services provided to the dog?"

"Yes, sir."

"Would you tell the court what the balance due is, as of today?"

"$850.00."

Swinton seems surprised by this, but he keeps going. "And it's true, isn't it, that most of that bill is the result of your treatment of Sherman for a broken foot?"

"More than half, yes sir."

"And the broken foot was the result of Mr. Hart's negligence, isn't that correct?"

Michelle Marvel jumps up, objects. Joe bobs forward. "Sustained."

Swinton rephrases: "Dr. Borden, what is your understanding of how the injury occurred?"

"A car swerved and hit Sherman."

"Who was with the dog when the injury occurred?"

"Mr. Hart, I believe."

"Was the dog on his leash at the time?"

"I don't think so, but according to what Mr. Hart told me, it wouldn't have made any difference."

"So I take it you're accepting Mr. Hart's version of what occurred at the time of the accident?"

The microphone picks up Tony Borden's sigh. He looks up at Joe. "You know, Judge, I don't want to take sides. This whole thing," and now he looks back at me, "makes me uncomfortable." He's a nice guy. I want to protect him. And I can't help noticing once again—though I caution myself it is absolutely, totally irrelevant—how sexy he is. Is this some special hell, custom-made for the three of us: my crazy ex-husband, this vet, and me?

"I appreciate that, Dr. Borden," says Joe, "but you'll have to answer Mr. Swinton's questions."

Swinton continues: "What were the charges for treatment of the broken foot?"

"$530."

"Thank you, I have no further questions."

Then it's Michelle Marvel's turn. "Dr. Borden,

if your total unpaid bill is now eight hundred thirty dollars, what was the remaining amount for?"

Tony Borden looks down at his records. "Five nights boarding, at fifty dollars per night, plus fifty dollars for treatment of dermatitis."

"Dermatitis?"

"Sherman had a rash."

"And what caused the rash, in your opinion?"

"I suspected it was the shampoo. Mrs. Hart had tried a new shampoo."

"Not one you recommend, is that right?"

"No, but I'm sure she didn't think it would do any harm. Like I say, I really don't want to get in the middle—"

"And the five nights boarding, were they consecutive?"

"No. Five separate nights."

"Five separate nights—over what period of time?"

Tony Borden studies his file. "The last two months."

"And who brought Sherman in for boarding?"

"Mrs. Hart."

"Prior to the past few months, did you ever board Sherman?"

"She and Mr. Hart brought him in once . . . It was a couple of years ago, before this . . . I think they went to Florida. We kept him less than a week."

"So, it's fair to say, then, Dr. Borden, that prior to the past two months, Sherman was not accustomed to being boarded?"

"I guess you could say that."

"And when Mrs. Hart brought Sherman in on the five occasions during the past two months, did she tell you why she needed to board him?"

"No, she just asked that we keep him overnight."

"Dr. Borden, are you aware of the schedule the court has put into effect, with regard to the parties' time with Sherman?"

"I know they share him. I don't know the details."

"Mr. Hart has Sherman on Wednesday afternoon for several hours, and every weekend. Mrs. Hart has him the rest of the time."

"That sounds like what she told me. Mrs. Hart, I mean."

"Have you ever suggested to Mrs. Hart that instead of leaving Sherman with you, she might let Mr. Hart keep him?" Michelle touches Mr. Hart's shoulder, a practiced gesture.

"I'm trying not to get in the middle—"

"But you're concerned with Sherman's welfare, aren't you?" Michelle asks. I can tell from the way she throws her shoulders back that she's happy with the way this is going, and then she says, her voice saturated with what, if you didn't know her, would sound like sincerity,

"Thank you, Dr. Borden. And although I had nothing to do with it, I apologize that you were summoned to court today on such short notice."

My ex-husband looks back at me. "Ms. Baynard, do you have any questions of this witness?" Tony Borden looks at his watch. He's been here almost an hour already.

I hadn't thought of it until now, but I see an opportunity. "Yes, your honor. Dr. Borden, I hand you a copy of an affidavit you signed yesterday, and which I filed with the clerk this morning. Would you read it, please?"

The affidavit is short, to the point. It ends with the sentence "I believe it is in Sherman's best interest that the court determine his permanent custodial arrangement as soon as possible, and I therefore support the guardian ad litem's motion to bifurcate."

"Your honor," I continue, "While this motion has not yet been scheduled, since we are all here this morning, I request that you consider it. I can't imagine why either party would object."

I can't imagine, but of course they do. Swinton and Marvel jump up together, protesting: ". . . insufficient notice . . . need time to consider . . . very unusual motion . . . not to be lightly granted . . ."

I cut them off. "Your honor, my motion is designed to protect Sherman's interests by allowing the court to issue an order as to his permanent custody without waiting for a trial on all the other matters. I think it makes perfect sense. I trust that nobody here wants the dog to suffer."

From an almost prone position in his chair—he's leaning so far back his voice seems to come out of nowhere—my ex says, "Dr. Borden, is the dog suffering?"

"Like I told her, not exactly. I think Sherman is coping, but—"

Joe bobs forward, swivels to face the vet. "Try to be a little more specific, Doctor. Told whom?"

"Sally . . . I mean Ms. Baynard."

"You know Ms. Baynard personally?"

"I don't know how to answer that." Tony Borden looks miserable.

"It's a fairly simple question," says Joe.

"We had dinner together, and I went over to her condo, but I wouldn't say we know each other well."

"Whose idea was that?"

"Excuse me?"

"The dinner, and the visit to her condo."

"Mine, I guess. But you don't understand—"

"Don't interrupt me, please."

"Yes, sir."

"I want you to be perfectly candid with me, Dr. Borden. I remind you that you are under oath."

"Yes, sir."

"How long have you known Ms. Baynard personally?"

I can't stand this any longer. "Judge, this is outrageous! My relationship with Dr. Borden has been perfectly—"

"Your *relationship?*" asks Joe.

"Professional," I finish, but he's not listening to me.

"That's correct, Judge," the vet pipes in. "I didn't mean to imply . . ."

"You don't have to imply anything," says Joe. "The facts speak for themselves." He glares at me. "Ms. Baynard, I caution you to limit your interactions with Dr. Borden to matters relating directly to the dog whose welfare it is your duty to protect. And while I'm inclined to deny your motion, I'll entertain any supporting legal authority you might provide, as well as anything Ms. Marvel and Mr. Swinton wish to submit. Is there anything further?"

Henry Swinton rises. "Your honor, what about our motion regarding the vet's bill?"

"Denied. That matter can wait until the trial."

Outside the courtroom Tony Borden says, "I guess that didn't go too well."

"It was a disaster."

"I'm sorry if I said something I shouldn'' have . . ."

I want to say, *Yes, you said a lot you shouldn'*

have, but instead, "It wasn't your fault. I don't know what's gotten into him, but we shouldn't be discussing this."

"What should we be discussing?"

"You heard the judge. We can discuss Sherman. That's all. I need to get back to my office." I start toward the elevator, leaving him standing outside the courtroom. I've almost made my escape when I hear the noise. Tony Borden, Michelle Marvel, and Henry Swinton have all disappeared, but there among the deadbeat dads are Mr. and Mrs. Hart, scuffling.

Mrs. Hart: "No, you can't have him early!"

Mr. Hart, yelling: "Don't yell!"

Mrs.: "Take your hands off me!"

Mr., louder: "Then quit slapping me!"

Mrs.: "You're a monster!"

I hold the elevator open and watch, as best I can through the crowd of men, all now craning for a view, as the deputies pull the Harts away from each other. *Stay out of this,* I tell myself, but I can't.

"She your client?" asks the deputy holding Mrs. Hart.

"No, but I'll be happy to talk to them, if you have an empty room somewhere . . ."

Mr. Hart, breathless: "I just asked her if I could have Sherman a little early today, even offered to drive out there to pick him up."

Mrs. Hart, screaming: "You'll be lucky if you

195

ever see him again!" She grabs the deputy's ear. "Let go of me!"

"Calm down, ma'am, or we'll have to put you in the lock-up. Ms. Baynard, you got any suggestions?"

"I think you should let Judge Baynard deal with them."

He deserves it, I say to myself as I head toward the elevator.

Mr. Adorable

A nything urgent here?" I ask Gina when I get back to the office.

"Derwood Carter called again, insists on talking to you. He doesn't have a lawyer, says he's going to represent himself. Says his wife—here, I wrote down his exact words—has mental problems."

"Because she wants to divorce him? I'd say that's a sign of perfect mental health."

"And he suggested you come to Beaufort to see if you two can't work out a settlement before you file anything. Lot of nerve, huh? I told him your schedule's really crammed in the next couple of weeks, but you'd be happy to meet with him here, next time he's holding court in Charleston."

"He has no intention of settling. He just wants to throw me off my game, delay while he tries to hide some assets."

"I looked over your notes and drafted a complaint. I didn't name the court reporter—you know, the one he's supposed to be bonking—so you might want to look at that paragraph. Here. And I wasn't sure about whether you wanted to ask for a change of venue."

"Absolutely. We can't try their case in Beaufort County."

"By the way, did you ask the Harts about their daughter?"

"I forgot. There was too much else going on."

"Did you remember to file the motion to bifurcate?"

"I left it with the clerk, but I think Judge Baynard's already decided to deny it."

"How can he deny it when it hasn't even been scheduled yet?" Gina asks.

"It's a long story. I'm too tired to explain it right now." The truth is, I'm too embarrassed to explain it. "But he wants us to file briefs on the legal issues. Can you start on the research?"

"Sure, I'm getting ready to order some lunch. Want a salad?"

"Sure, thanks."

I close the door to my office and do something I hardly ever do: I stretch out on my sofa and close my eyes. I want to forget about *Hart v. Hart*. Forget about Joe Baynard, forget Tony Borden. I want to forget about my mother losing her mind and Delores leaving. I want to make the headache go away.

When Gina knocks I have to jerk myself out of a dream—I'm lying on a towel on the beach, my body somehow restored to its twenty-something smoothness, and I have the beach all to myself—

when I hear her say, "Don't worry, Mr. Adorable, I know she'll be happy to see *you!*" Who is she talking to?

"Just a minute," I say, sitting up, straightening my blouse.

"I brought your salad," Gina says, "and look who else!"

There's Sherman, right behind her. He seems very interested in the plastic bag that holds my lunch.

"What's he doing here?"

"One of the court deputies dropped him off. And he comes with papers!" She hands me an envelope. Inside is this:

In the Family Court for
the Ninth Judicial Circuit
Case No. 1901
Maryann S. Hart, Plaintiff v.
Russell B. Hart, Defendant

ORDER

It appears to this Court that the parties to this case are unable to communicate peacefully regarding their pet, Sherman, and that it is in Sherman's best interest to be placed in a neutral environment; therefore, it is hereby

Ordered, that Sherman be immediately placed in the custody of his Guardian,

Sarah B. Baynard, Esq., until a trial in this case, and it is further

Ordered, that the parties are hereby restrained from any contact, whether in person, by telephone, or electronically, with each other, except as supervised by Ms. Baynard, and that they shall be allowed visitation with Sherman only as supervised by Ms. Baynard.

And it is so Ordered.

The Honorable Joseph Baynard,
Chief Administrative Judge

"This isn't funny," I say.

"It's not a joke. The deputy said the Harts created quite a ruckus over there. Your judge—"

"Quit calling him that!"

"*The* judge sent the deputy out to Mrs. Hart's house to pick up the dog. There's a bag of his stuff on my desk: some food, toys, . . . a leash, some medicine, other stuff." At the sound of the word "food" Sherman's ears perk up. "You hungry, Mr. Adorable?"

"I can't take care of him. It's impossible."

"What's impossible about it? He'll be fine here during office hours . . . I can look out for him . . . and you'll just take him home at night. He's perfectly well-behaved, aren't you, Sherman?"

"I've got enough to deal with at home, without a damn dog." At this, Sherman flinches, hangs his head. "Gina," I say in my sweetest voice, "you'd love to have him for a while, wouldn't you?"

"Of course I'd love to take him, but the order doesn't say *me,* it says *you.*"

"What will I do with him at home?"

"They'll let you have a dog in your building, won't they?"

"That's not the point."

"And your mother will love him," she says. "Just try it for a night or two. You know what I think?"

"What?"

"I think this may be Judge Baynard's way of getting them to settle."

"No, he's punishing me."

"For what?"

I tell her about the hearing. Every time I say "vet," Sherman's ears perk up.

"Wow, so your judge is really jealous, huh? The poor guy must really be crazy for you. And the vet likes you, too."

"What makes you think that?"

"Because when I took the affidavit out to him, he asked me how long you'd been divorced."

"That doesn't mean anything."

"And when I said 'it was a long time ago, but I don't think she's completely over it—'"

"What in hell did you say that for?" I'm scaring Sherman. His tail, normally held high, drops down behind his legs, and he disappears behind the sofa.

"You want the whole truth and nothing but the truth?" Gina says. "First, because it's true: You aren't over it. Isn't that why you've never let anybody else have a chance, because you're still mourning over Joe Baynard?" Gina's voice has that high-pitched shakiness it gets when she's confronting me, not as employee to employer but as girlfriend to girlfriend. "And second, since I'm being honest, because I guess I was hoping I'd discourage him."

"So you could work your wiles on him, right?" I sound as mean as I feel. I don't blame Sherman for staying behind the sofa.

"Yes, but don't worry, he doesn't seem the slightest bit interested. Maybe he's as screwed up as you are—still mourning over *his* divorce!"

"Gina," I say, trying to stay calm, though she doesn't deserve it, "I need you to act like a secretary, not a high-school sophomore."

"Sure," she says sarcastically. "May I get you a cup of coffee, Ms. Baynard?"

I should fire her, but how do you fire one of your best friends? "Just leave me alone!"

When Gina flees I call my other real friend, Ellen. She's going over police reports in a nasty rape case and is glad for the distraction. "You have any books on dogs?" I ask.

"You didn't get out of that case?"

202

"No. I'm in even deeper now."

"Why are you laughing?"

"I guess I'm losing it." But it feels good to laugh. Only now does Sherman decide it's safe to reappear.

I open the back door of my car, move some things I've been meaning to take to the dry cleaners, and pat the seat. "Hop in, Sherman." He doesn't budge. "What's the matter? Too good for a Toyota?" I pick him up, plop him on the seat. I'm just pulling out of the parking lot onto Broad Street when I feel his nose nudging my elbow—an insistent nudge—and he hops through the space between the front seats and then onto the passenger side, where he seems satisfied. "Okay, I get it. I didn't mean to insult you by making you sit in the back."

When I pull into the cavernous darkness of the condo parking garage he stands up in the seat, presses his nose against the window. "Don't worry," I assure him, "I don't live down here. You'll see, it isn't so bad." I'm not sure who I'm consoling—Sherman or myself.

He hesitates as I lead him—*yes, Mrs. Hart, he's on his leash*—past the front desk and into the elevator. "What's his name?" asks a woman I recognize from my floor. Before today, we've only nodded at each other.

"Sherman."

"He's very handsome," she says. Sherman sniffs around her feet, then up her leg.

"Stop that, Sherman!" I scold.

"He smells Curly. My poodle. Maybe you'd like to walk with us sometime?"

"He's just staying with me temporarily," I explain.

"Oh, that's a shame. I don't see how you're going to part with him!"

Sherman seems happy to see Delores—could he remember her from the beach?—but she's definitely not happy to see him. "We don't need no animal around here. That judge must be crazy!"

"He's not thinking straight. Marital problems."

"Should have learned his lesson the first time around," she says. Delores knows the bare bones of the Joe-Sally story. "You!" she shouts at Sherman. "Get away from that trash can!"

"He's just confused right now."

"Who? The dog or the judge?"

"The judge. The dog, too, probably."

"Was he that crazy when you were married to him?" she asks.

"No. We were just too different." I unpack the bag of Sherman's supplies. "Delores, do you think I should put some gravy or something on this food? It looks so boring." Sherman dances around me, his eyes intent on the plastic bowl.

"Gravy might give him the runs. Fancy dogs like this, they got sensitive stomachs."

Sherman devours the dry food without any hesitation. "I wonder if I gave him enough," I say, squinting to read the directions on the bag of food.

"If the judge wanted to put this animal in a foster home, he should have picked somebody who knows about dogs." Delores fills another bowl with water. "And you're gonna have to take him outside later, so he can do his business. I don't want to be cleaning up after no animal."

"Where's Mom?"

"Sleeping," says Delores.

"She's sleeping a lot lately."

"I try to keep her up, but after a while she just don't have the energy."

"What did she eat today?"

"A couple of bites of spaghetti, a little bit of salad. Not enough to keep a bird alive. We took a walk, but she can't go far, and then we came back and tried to watch a movie, but she couldn't keep up with the story. I think it wore her out." She gathers her purse and coat. "You been thinking about what we talked about?"

"I haven't had much time."

"Charlie's about to have his first chemo treatment."

"Maybe things will go better than you think."

"The doctor says it might buy him a few

months, but not much more. It's gonna be rough."

"I know you need to be with him, Delores. I've made a couple appointments to look at some nursing homes," I say. I feel like a traitor to Mom.

After Delores leaves, Sherman follows me back to the bedroom, where I change into a sweatshirt and jeans and he explores the jumble of shoes at the bottom of my closet. He's well past puppyhood but I sense that he's nostalgic for chewing, and I give him an old sandal with a broken strap. "Here, Mr. Adorable. Make yourself at home."

I can't remember the last time I wore the sandals. They're white, delicate, not the kind of thing I'd ever wear to work. They belong to another time, long ago, maybe some garden party with Joe. The strap's been broken for years. "Fix them or throw them away," my mother would say, if she could.

Running in His Sleep

I've brought part of the Hart file home with me, but I'm not sure why. Maybe I want to believe in magic: maybe somewhere in these notes and memos there's an answer, a way out. That happens every now and then when I'm so immersed in a case that I'm drowning in facts. I'll read through my notes and remember what my old law school professor used to say: *Every case is a story. Ask yourself: What's essential in this story? Take that narrative and shape your strategy around it.*

Sherman's curled at my feet. He doesn't seem interested in the sandal. "You miss them, honey?" I say. He looks up, his eyes dark and brooding behind the heavy brows. "Maybe we should give them a call, let them know you're okay."

Mr. Hart doesn't answer, but I leave a message on his machine. Mrs. Hart doesn't pick up right away. She sounds a little drunk. "He's doing fine," I say. "I gave him some dinner, and now he's—"

"You don't need to feed him but once a day, in the morning," she snaps. "I put a note in the bag about all that."

"Oh, I'm sorry, I didn't see it. What about those pills in the little bottle?"

"Heartworm tablets. He needs one on the first of next month."

"I can't imagine I'll have him that long."

"Didn't you read the order? The judge said you're going to keep him until the trial. Henry Swinton says that could be six months or more." She's crying. Sherman hears her voice, hops onto the sofa next to me.

"If you and Mr. Hart would settle, we could get this over with tomorrow."

"How can we settle? We can't divide Sherman in half."

"No, but perhaps you could work out a schedule that would be acceptable to both of you. One of you could have primary custody, and the other—"

"What about poor Sherman? Should he spend the rest of his life going back and forth?"

"Mrs. Hart, I'm not your lawyer, but I'm sure Henry has told you how unpredictable these cases can be . . . I mean, when a case goes to trial, you lose control over the outcome. What happened today is just an example."

"What happened today was an abomination!" She struggles not to slur her words, pronouncing every syllable of *abomination* very carefully.

"My point is, wouldn't it be better to work out an agreement you can live with than to take a chance that you'd lose Sherman altogether?"

"I don't see how that can possibly happen." I hear her take a sip of something. "Where will he sleep tonight?"

"In my bedroom, I guess."

"He's accush-tomed to sleeping with me."

"Will he need to go out, to pee, before bed-time?"

"Yes. But you'll need an umbrella."

"What?"

"It's raining here," she says. "If it's raining there, he won't go out un-lesh you cover him with an umbrella."

"Mrs. Hart, I need to ask you about something else." I turn the pages of my notes. "It's about Anna."

There's a silence, then, "Anna has nothing to do with this case."

"Is she your daughter?"

"Anna has chosen not to have a relationship. I haven't seen her since she was eighteen."

"How old is she now?"

"Thirty . . . thirty-six."

"So you haven't seen your daughter in eighteen years?"

"It's her choice, not mine."

"I'd like to understand what happened."

"But it doesn't have anything to do with Sherman."

"Please, Mrs. Hart. You have to let me decide what's relevant and what's not."

She sighs. "Anna was a difficult child. Brilliant, very artistic, but headstrong. When she was fifteen—a rising junior in high school—she convinced Rusty to let her apply to the Governor's School for the Arts."

"It's up in Greenville, right?"

"Yes. A public boarding school. I knew it would be a mistake. The students were . . . I don't know . . . They were just too . . . and I didn't want Anna living two hundred miles from home, but Rusty wouldn't listen. Things went better than I expected her first year there, then in her senior year she came home for Christmas break and she just wasn't herself."

"In what way?"

"She didn't want to tell me, but I found out. She'd fallen in love with a boy from Newberry. They were having sex."

"It happens."

"It may happen to other people's children, but I was determined it wasn't going to happen to Anna. Not in *high school,* for good-nesh sake. So Rusty and I drove up there and confronted the head-master. He suggested we talk to her about birth control and, oh, you know, the other unpleasant things . . . I was furious. I insisted he give us the address of the boy's parents, and on the way back to Columbia, Rusty and I paid a call on them. They lived in a trailer park. The father worked as a common laborer. They weren't our kind of people. They were polite, said they would talk to him, but I could just tell from their environment that they'd have no control over him."

"But if he made it to the Governor's School, he must have been a pretty special kid, right?"

"Talent is not the shame . . . same . . . as character," Mrs. Hart says. "I think I hear Sherman whining."

"He's fine. He's right here."

"Anyway, after this episode Rusty and I had a big argument. I wanted to take her out of that school right away. He wanted her to stay. Finally he came to his right mind."

"She had only a semester left before graduation, right?"

"We—I—arranged for her to transfer to Pharington's, in Richmond. They agreed to take her on condition that she repeat her senior year."

"How did she react to that?"

"Not well. She blamed me for being too controlling. She blamed her father for not standing up to me. But then she calmed down, and we thought everything was . . . Excuse me, I need a tissue. This is so difficult . . . We thought everything was going to work out. We took her to Pharington's. She was acting a little strange—not yelling anymore, but just too quiet. The next thing we know, we get a call from the headmistress that she's run away. And she hasn't come home since."

"You haven't talked to her at all?"

"She communicates with Rusty, but he's very

211

secretive about it. He may even have seen her a couple of times, in New York."

"She lives in New York?"

"I think so. Rusty slipped up once after a business trip to Manhattan, said something about having gone to an art gallery. He NEVER goes to art galleries, so I was quite suspicious. And he's still going to New York at least twice a year, even though he's retired. He never wants me to come along. Says he visits one of his old banking buddies, but I don't believe him."

"Surely if he'd seen her, if he'd talked to her, he'd tell you," I say.

"You would think so, if he had a shred of decency . . ." She's crying. "Now do you see this has nothing whatsoever to do with Sherman?"

"I appreciate your being honest with me, Mrs. Hart."

"Sherman is the only one in my life, the only one who's been loyal."

"He's a good dog."

"When can I see him?"

"What about tomorrow morning, at my office? I'll be busy, but Gina will be there."

"Perhaps I could take him out for a walk?"

"No, I'm sorry, Mrs. Hart. I can't disobey the order."

When we hang up, I check on my mother. Sherman follows me into the dark room. The steady drone of her snoring is almost lost in the sound of the rain against the window.

Years from now, when I'm an old woman like my mother, even if I've forgotten almost everything else, I'm sure I'll remember standing in the downpour outside my building, rain running in sheets down my parka, holding an umbrella over Sherman, who's taking his sweet time. And I'll remember sharing my bed with this little fellow who runs in his sleep, holding him until he settles down.

Neutered

I apologize for yesterday," says Gina.
    "So do I."

We're like two old married people. They always argue, but even while they're arguing, they know they're going to make up—unless, of course, they're the Harts.

"I guess you slowed her down this morning, huh?" she says to Sherman. It's already nine thirty. I usually beat Gina to the office.

"No, it was my mother. She wanted to keep him. Had a fit when I tried to leave."

"Henry Swinton called. So did Michelle Marvel. They're considering asking for an emergency hearing—for a stay—before the supreme court. They want to know if you'll join in the petition."

"It's nice to know they're agreeing on something for a change, but the South Carolina Supreme Court's not going to touch this with a ten-foot pole. And anyway, somebody would have to move for a stay before Judge Baynard first."

"That doesn't make any sense. Why would he stay an order he just issued?"

"It doesn't make much sense, but those are the rules. You have to give the trial judge a chance to correct his own mistakes. If he won't, then you can ask the higher court for relief, but even then they won't grant a hearing unless they feel that some irreparable harm is going to occur as a result of the order. Remember, this isn't a final order. The Supremes try to discourage appeals from intermediate orders."

"So what do you want me to tell them? Michelle and Henry."

"Tell them I'll look over their materials."

"And Mr. Vogel's lawyer sent another motion for continuance. Mr. Vogel still can't get around, even with crutches. I called Mrs. Vogel. She had a hissy, says he's always been a . . . what was her word . . . I wrote it down . . . here . . . a 'malingerer'. She doesn't want you to consent to the continuance. I explained to her that he's got a surgeon's affidavit, but she wants to talk to you. And Rick Silber's coming in to review his interrogatories."

"Maryann Hart will be in around ten," I say. "I told her she could visit with Sherman for a while. Can you kind of watch over them?"

"You don't think she'd kidnap him, do you?"

"No, but I'm supposed to be 'supervising,' whatever that means."

"Sure. We'll have a good time, won't we, Sherman? I just happen to have something for you." She reaches into her desk drawer, pulls out a bag of dog chews. "Sit! That's a good boy!"

"And by the way, you were right." I say. "Anna is their daughter."

"I told you."

Rick Silber is wearing his usual sandals with white socks. And he does the usual, which is to take off the sandals and sit cross-legged on my sofa, like he's in some kind of yoga position. I wonder if he does this with his patients, but then I remember he doesn't have patients—he just teaches psychology.

"It's not really the interrogatories I need to talk to you about," he says.

"Well, we need to get those done."

"I know. I'm working on the answers."

"I thought Gina said you were almost finished."

"Yeah, that's what I want to talk to you about. Gina." He pulls at his goatee, twists the tip of it into a little point. Someone should tell him the goatee looks ridiculous on his baby-smooth, pale face, but it won't be me. "She's really terrific," he says.

"Yes, she's very smart. I keep telling her she should go to law school."

"No, I mean she's a terrific *person,* in every respect."

"She's good with people."

"You didn't tell her about my problem, did you?"

"Which problem?"

"The . . . uh . . . kind of personal issue."

"Of course not."

"And you didn't put it in your notes, did you?"

"I don't think so."

"Good. Because I'd like to have a chance with her. Would that be okay with you?"

"Rick, I'm not in charge of Gina's social life."

"It wouldn't piss you off—if I asked her out?"

"Not at all, but you'd better wait until your case is over."

"We could just go out to dinner, couldn't we? I promise I'll behave myself."

"Is that all you wanted to talk about today?"

"Yes." He looks at his watch. "Didn't take long, did it? But I guess you're still going to charge me."

I've been patient so far, but now I can't help myself. "Rick, I'm going to give you some advice about Gina."

"What's that?"

"She doesn't put up with a lot of nonsense. She knows what she wants, and she's not interested in men who need parenting."

"So, in other words," he says, "not me."

"That's not what I said. I think you're fully capable of being a grown-up." I'm not at all sure about this, but I figure I'll give him some hope.

"So, I have your permission to ask her out to dinner?"

"I'm not your mother, I'm your lawyer. Your

217

lawyer advises you to wait until your case is over." But even as I say this, I can tell he's only hearing what he wants to hear.

By the time Rick leaves and I've talked to Mrs. Vogel, explained that there's nothing we can do about the second continuance—her husband's leg hasn't healed, he's still in a lot of pain—and calmed her down, it's almost lunch time. Maryann Hart is still with Sherman in the waiting room. He's asleep in her lap.

"He looks like he's gained weight," she whispers when I come in. "Remember not to feed him more than once a day, in the morning. And he needs his exercise. I'd be happy to walk him today."

"I'm sorry, but I'm not supposed to let you—"

"That judge is out of his mind!" she interrupts, not whispering now, and Sherman's eyes open with a start. "No wonder you divorced him! Henry Swinton says he's going end up losing his job, the way he's behaving."

I don't want to continue this conversation. "Mrs. Hart, I'm glad you had a chance to visit with Sherman this morning, but I have a lunch appointment, so I'm going to have to excuse myself."

"But if you're going to be busy, I could stay a little longer . . ."

"No, I'm taking Sherman with me."

"Please remember to keep him on the leash," she says. And to Sherman: "Darling, I know this is hard on you, but be a good boy. We'll be back together soon, I promise!" There are tears in her eyes. I have to hold Sherman to keep him from following her.

My "lunch appointment" isn't really an appointment, and it isn't lunch. I want to check on Mr. Hart. He hasn't returned my phone call from last night, nor Gina's this morning. Sherman and I head down Broad Street, turn left on Meeting toward the Battery. It's a gorgeous day, everything washed clean by the rain, the street at least temporarily relieved of the accumulated stench from the horse-drawn carriages that carry tourists through the historic neighborhood. Charleston is always beautiful, green and lush even in the fall, the formal gardens always blooming with something. We pass the house where Joe lives—or used to live—with Susan, a brick antebellum with white columns and a circular driveway behind a wrought-iron gate. It's lovely, not pompous but dignified, like one of those old Charleston ladies who sit in the front row at church.

"You like this house?" I ask Sherman. He looks up at me, wondering why we're stopping. "They probably have a dog." But I don't know for sure. Joe and I have been friendly all these years, exchanging pleasantries at bar association social events and in court, but never, until recently, risking anything beyond that. He's never confided any unhappiness beyond the predictable rants about his job—how it's his fate to be stuck in the family court forever—or occasional complaints about the adolescent exploits of his boys, complaints uttered with a smile, more like a proud father's preening.

It occurs to me, as I stand in front of his house, that I don't know much about Joe at all anymore, nor he about me, and maybe that's why it's been so easy for both of us to sustain our fantasies.

Sherman lets out a little bark, as if to say, *Let's get going!* We continue down Meeting Street past the Calhoun Mansion and take a left on South Battery. The breeze is strong enough to send sprays across the battery wall and the smell of sea creatures rides the damp air. Now the dog knows where he is; his little legs move along the sidewalk so fast he's pulling me behind him. Outside the Harts' house he heads toward the shrubbery to the left of the front porch, and when I try to drag him back, he barks a sharp protest, so I give him some leash. He comes out with a newspaper in his mouth. "Good boy," I say. It's this morning's *Post and Courier*.

When Mr. Hart doesn't come to the door after several rings of the doorbell, I think the worst, but then he appears in his bathrobe, unshaven, the long strands of his usual comb-over falling down across one ear. He looks as if he's been sleeping for days. He takes a minute to adjust his glasses before he recognizes me. The scowl on his face isn't welcoming, but when he sees Sherman with the newspaper he grins and lets us in.

"You can take him off that damn leash, now," he says, and I do. The dog runs in circles around him, sliding on the polished wood floor.

"You didn't return my call," I explain. "I was worried."

"Sorry. Guess I thought it would be more bad news."

"I just wanted to let you see he's okay."

He picks the dog up. Sherman licks his face. I notice they both have the same bushy eyebrows. "I guess I should be polite and ask you to sit down," he says to me. "Excuse my appearance."

I follow him into the formal parlor and we sit across from each other, Mr. Hart on the delicate Victorian sofa that groans under his weight, Sherman beside him. "She'd have a fit if she could see you on this thing," he says to the dog. "But go ahead, get it dirty. I don't give a damn."

"Your wife had a visit with him this morning," I say. "So I thought it only fair . . ."

"There's nothing fair about this whole business."

"It wasn't my idea."

"But it's not so bad, is it? You get paid two

hundred fifty dollars an hour and you end up with Sherman!"

"This is just a temporary arrangement. And again, it wasn't my idea."

"You stretch the case out long enough, you make a fortune, and soon enough my boy here won't even remember me."

"Mr. Hart, I'm doing everything I can do to expedite the case." I pull out my legal pad. "Your wife told me about Anna. She thinks you're in contact with her. I'd like her phone number."

"You don't need to talk to Anna."

"I'm trying to be thorough."

"If you want to be thorough, you can find out where my wife goes at night. She leaves the house several times a week, always at night, stays away for an hour or two."

"If you're really that interested, you should talk to your lawyer."

"I'm interested, but I don't want to pay a detective. I'm sure I'll end up paying for Maryann's spy before it's all over. So do me a favor, ask her where she goes."

"I will, if you'll give me Anna's number."

"Anna left home long before we got Sherman."

"I know that, but I want to talk to her. Will you give me the number?"

"I'll have to look for it. I'll call your office." He rubs a spot under Sherman's chin and the dog turns on his back, begging for a stomach rub.

"Why did you lie on your counterclaim, about Anna?"

"I didn't lie, I just didn't contradict my wife when she wrote that we had no children."

"I think there's more to it than that."

"It's what she insists we tell people when they ask. 'No children.' I guess she almost made me believe it myself."

"But you see your daughter, don't you?"

"Once in a blue moon."

"So, I'm going to tell Anna you gave me her number, if that's okay."

"What choice do I have? I'm like this poor little guy." He rubs Sherman's belly again. "Neutered. That's what Maryann's done to us, isn't it, buddy?"

"I need to get back to my office. You promise you'll call with the number?"

"If a promise means anything anymore," he says, "I promise."

Golden Memories

Delores is surprised to see me home so early, and she ignores Sherman, who prances into the kitchen a couple of steps ahead of me, as if he's lived here all his life. "Your mama's been napping close to two hours now. I was about to wake her up, or she won't sleep tonight."

"I talked to her doctor, got the names of some nursing homes. I'd like to visit one this afternoon, if you wouldn't mind looking after Sherman." The dog is over by the trash can, circling it, sampling all its olfactory offerings.

"We going to be stuck with this dog forever?"

"It's not his fault."

"The way you been acting with that dog, seems like you want to hold onto him," she says.

"That's not an option, even if I wanted to."

"When's the last time he did his business?"

"What? Oh, just a few minutes ago."

"I don't like him, but I'll watch him." Sherman's ears droop, as if he understands the insult, and he heads back toward my mother's room. "Now your mama, she sure does love that animal." It occurs to me that Delores, despite her protestations, might be falling for Sherman, too.

• • •

There must be a national committee of insipid people who choose the names for nursing homes: Loving Hands, Golden Memories, Compassionate Care. The one closest to the condo, Golden Memories, is across the bridge in Mt. Pleasant, only ten minutes away. There's an impressive stone entrance gate opening onto a well-kept complex of buildings. The main building is faux colonial, with white columns and a row of rocking chairs on the wide front porch, but the chairs are all empty.

"Let me see if someone in our marketing department is available," says the woman at the front desk. "We usually work by appointment . . ."

"This has come up rather unexpectedly," I say.

"Have a seat, and I'll see if I can find . . . Here, you can look over this packet and start filling out the forms."

"But I'm not quite ready to—"

"I know, honey. Nobody's ever ready, but we need some information about your loved one before we can get the process started."

"It's my mother."

"And for your loved one, would you be wanting assisted living, nursing, or the dementia unit?"

If she says "loved one" again, I'll leave. "I don't know."

"Okay, like I said, you just go ahead and fill

out the forms, and I'll see if I can find someone in marketing."

But I don't want to talk to marketing. She turns her back and I escape her, walking as fast as I can through the double doors, which spring open, set in motion by a man in a gray uniform who pushes a cart of cleaning supplies and who doesn't seem to care about intruders. I find myself at one end of a long hall I can't see the end of, with rooms on either side, the names of the inhabitants written with erasable marker on name plates on the doors. Now and then a door is open and I can peek inside. Violet McCarter (orange marker, smiley face beside the name) is in bed, asleep, TV blaring. Sam Schumaker (blue marker, no smiley face) sits in a recliner, staring out into space. The place smells almost too clean, as if everything remotely biological has been extinguished. The framed pictures on the walls are the pictorial equivalent of Muzak—pastel florals and idyllic landscapes.

But it's not so bad here, I tell myself, not like that place I saw once in a newspaper exposé, with filthy floors and pock-marked walls, where old people with haunted faces wasted away in their beds.

"May I help you?" says another person in a gray uniform.

"I'm visiting my aunt." I point down the hall.

"We ask all our visitors to wear a name tag,"

she says, smiling. "Please try to remember next time. It's for the protection of your loved one."

I turn a corner, thinking maybe I should leave— I'll need to talk to "marketing" and do more research if I'm serious about putting Mom here —when I come upon an old man in striped pajamas, sitting in a chair that swallows him.

"How are you?" I say in that way we do when we want to keep moving.

"Please." He grabs my hand. "You should come more often."

"I think you're confusing me with someone else." His hand is thin, cold. He won't let go.

"Your brother doesn't come," he says. "Not since Christmas." Then he tries to stand, wobbles, falls back into the chair.

"I'll find someone to help you."

"*You* help me."

"What's your name?"

"Bird."

I remember passing his room a couple of doors back (Charles Bird, blue marker). "Would you like me to help you back to your room?" I help him get to his feet, his fingers pinching my arm as we make our way step by shaky step. When I have him safely in bed he grabs my hand again.

"You should come more," he says. "Tell your brother . . . tell him he always was a selfish SOB."

I flee, past marketing, past the front desk, into the late afternoon. Only when I'm outside do I realize how that sanitized air has lingered in my lungs, left me feeling like I can't breathe.

I'm on my way home, trying to imagine moving my mother into such a place, a place humming with good intentions, staffed with decent people doing the best they can, all pastels and florals and smiley faces, but still a place where Mr. Charles Bird sits alone, lost, only a few doors from his room. A place that is not, by any stretch of the imagination, likely to foster any golden memories.

I'm pulling into the condo garage when Gina calls. "Mr. Hart called to give you Anna's number. Want me to call her?"

"No, I'll do it."

My mother's asleep again when I get home, but at least she's eaten.

"Was it a nice place?" asks Delores.

"Not too bad, but I'm going to look at a couple more. Where's Sherman?"

"Back there in her room. Looks like she made a friend for life."

"What's that?" There's a circle of wet tile on the floor around Sherman's bowl. "She gave him some of her supper. You should have seen that animal, he just gobbled it up like nobody ever feeds him, but then he threw up."

"He's not supposed to eat people food."

"Guess she wanted to give him a special treat. I didn't have the heart to stop her."

"What was it?"

"Spaghetti and meatballs. He chewed up four big meatballs like they was nothing! Before I go, you should take him out, see if he'll do his business."

My mother's room is dark. Sherman's curled at the end of her bed; he winces when I pick him up. "Sorry, sweetheart," I whisper. "You have a stomachache?" I hold him as gently as I can until we're outside. There's a sign sticking up out of the grass, NO PETS IN THIS AREA, but I don't have time to take him to the park, so I let him down behind a big camellia bush. He curls his back and seems poised to go, but then he looks up at me as if to say, *I need my privacy!*

"Just hurry up, please." When he finishes he seems exhausted, so I carry him back upstairs and do my best to comfort him. "I'm sorry you don't feel good. We'll have a quiet night, okay?"

After Delores leaves I heat up some leftover vegetable soup and sit at the kitchen table with a stack of files. In the first months after my divorce I discovered this cure to eating alone: I invite my clients to dinner. It's almost as if they're in the room. I can work on their problems and feel useful.

Sherman's under the table, his head resting on

my feet. When he whimpers I lean down to make sure he's okay. One eye opens slowly but, as if focusing is too taxing, closes again. Maybe he's depressed. I wouldn't blame him. No one can explain to him what's happening, why he's in this strange place.

I review the draft of a divorce decree in one of my few uncomplicated cases, a short marriage with few assets, then open the Hart file. Henry Swinton and Michelle Marvel have filed cross-petitions asking Joe to stay his latest order. Michelle alleges that "the trial judge, in an attempt to punish the parties, is instead punishing their innocent pet." Swinton writes that "Sherman will suffer irreparable harm in the present custodial arrangement." He means me. Sherman whimpers again as if in agreement.

I make a list of witnesses: Mr. and Mrs., check. Dr. Borden, check. Mindy Greene, the next-door neighbor, check. I put a question mark next to Veronica, Mrs. Hart's maid, though it's unlikely she'll risk saying anything negative about her employer. An "X" next to Bill Falkner, the ex-cop detective Mrs. Hart hired—I don't need to watch the video of Rusty Hart kissing Mindy Greene. The last name on the list is Anna.

I'm a thousand miles away from New York City, but I feel like an intruder. "May I speak to Anna Hart, please?"

"May I ask who's calling?"

"This is Sarah Baynard. I'm a lawyer in Charleston, South Carolina. Is this Ms. Hart?" She doesn't answer, so I keep talking. "I'm sorry to bother you, but your parents are involved in some litigation—"

"I don't see why that concerns me." The voice is controlled, the words sharp and clipped, no hint of a southern drawl.

"Your parents are divorcing."

"I know that. Why they'd bother to divorce after all these years of being miserable together, I can't imagine, but I'm not going to get involved in their absurd little drama. My father has already asked me and I've—"

"I don't represent your father."

She laughs. "So, you're *her* lawyer?"

"I represent . . . The judge appointed me to protect the interests of their dog."

"Is this some kind of joke?"

"I just have a few questions . . ."

"Look, Ms.—"

"Baynard."

"Ms. Baynard, I haven't been in my parents' home for years. I haven't seen or spoken to my mother since I was eighteen. I have nothing—"

"But you talk to your father."

"Not often."

"I wonder if you would mind telling me what led you to become estranged from your mother?"

"Why don't you ask *her?*"

"She told me that you had some differences over a boy."

"Look, I've spent ten years and thousands of dollars with a therapist, and I can assure you it's much more complicated than 'differences over a boy.' But again, I'm not going to get involved in this. I can't believe they even *have* a dog."

"Why is that?"

"Because they never let *me* have one."

"Who, your mother or your father?"

"Both. They could never agree on anything. She wanted a little dog, he wanted a big dog. She wanted a purebred dog, he just wanted a dog."

"So Sherman is their first dog?"

"I have no idea. Like I told you, I haven't been home in years. Is someone hurting the dog?"

"Not that I'm aware of."

"Because you said something about protecting the dog . . ."

"Right. I'm kind of like a guardian for the dog appointed by the court. Your parents both want him."

"That figures."

"They both love him very much."

"So to show him how much they love him, they fight over him, right? Sounds familiar."

"I'm not sure I'm following you."

"In all these years they've never figured out how to share anything. They couldn't even share me. My mother wanted total loyalty from me which in her mind meant I wasn't allowed to admire anything about my father. My father was just as pathetic in his own way. He didn't want me to grow up to be like her, so he was constantly criticizing her to me, undermining her. They didn't have a clue how to raise a child. And now I guess they're doing the same thing to the dog. I'm sorry, I'm afraid I have to go."

"Just a couple more questions. When your father talked to you about the divorce, he didn't mention the dog?"

"No."

"And has he ever mentioned the dog in any of your other conversations?"

"Not that I remember. We don't talk very often. Look, I have to go. I have to pick my daughter up from the babysitter."

"Your father didn't tell me he had a grandchild."

"Because he doesn't know. I'm not going to let him become involved in my child's life, so why hurt his feelings? He and I have lunch here in the city once a year or so. We're not close. Besides, he wouldn't approve."

"Approve of what?"

"I'm a single mother. I know what he thinks about—as he would put it—'children born out of wedlock.' And let me be clear: It isn't just my father. My mother's just as bad, in her own way. The combination is lethal. They've never agreed on anything."

"So, I guess that answers my last question."

"Which is?"

"Do you think your parents could learn to cooperate in sharing custody of the dog?" Silence on the other end of the phone. "I'm sorry I had to bother you about this."

"Ms. Baynard?"

"Yes?"

"What I told you about my daughter is confidential."

"I don't see why I would have to bring it up."

"And if my father has some idea about calling me as a witness, you can tell him it's not a very good idea. What I'd have to say wouldn't help him. It wouldn't help either one of them. I feel sorry for the poor dog."

"Sherman seems to be holding his own."

"You know what?" Her voice is acid with sarcasm. "Maybe the dog should divorce *them.* Find a new home."

After the phone call I feel sick, as if the Harts—Mr., Mrs., and now Anna—have somehow infected me with their anger and sadness. Even Sherman, poor fellow, seems to be succumbing. He's lethargic, not exactly sleeping but not fully awake, either. Every few minutes he whimpers and his whole body jerks. His nose feels warm. I take him back to my bedroom, settle him on the bed, lie down beside him.

"I'm sorry," I say, stroking his back.

What am I apologizing for? None of this is my fault. I didn't break up the Harts' marriage or screw up their relationship with Anna. I didn't ask for this case. I'm not responsible for Joe's midlife crisis, if that's what it is. I didn't ask for custody of this little dog. *No,* I tell myself, *it isn't your fault,* but I can't shake the feeling that maybe it is. As if to comfort me, Sherman nuzzles into my neck. Each time he exhales his whiskers tickle me a little, but I don't mind.

A Memo to the File

The howl seems to come from a wild beast, a cry from the darkness, but when it wakes me I realize it's right here, beside me. Sherman. He's in pain.

There's nothing to do but call the vet. I dial the emergency number and he answers on the third ring, sleepily: "Tony Borden." Just hearing his voice calms me. He listens as I describe the symptoms.

"He's quiet now," I explain, "but he just isn't . . . He's not acting like himself. I was going to call you in the morning but—"

"Can you bring him to the clinic?"

I check my watch. It's 2:00 a.m. Delores won't be here for another six hours. "I can't leave my mother."

"It'll take me half an hour to get there. What's the gate code? I don't think I kept it."

"Should I be doing anything?"

"See if he'll take some water, but otherwise just try to keep him quiet, and don't feed him anything."

Almost as soon as I hang up, Sherman seems better. He follows me around as I check on my mother—she's managed to sleep through this—and change into jeans and a T-shirt. He's right behind me in the kitchen as I start a pot of coffee. He even seems interested in his empty food bowl looking up at me expectantly, cocking his head as if to say, *Where's my breakfast?*

"Maybe I overreacted," I say when I open the door for Dr. Borden. "He seems a lot better now."

"Let me take a look at him. Come here, boy. It's okay." I watch as the vet examines him, gently probing his abdomen, listening with the stethoscope. Sherman stays amazingly still, as if he knows he needs this.

"What have you been feeding him?" he asks.

"Maryann Hart gave me a bag of that dry stuff. But while I was gone my mother gave him some meatballs. He threw up."

"That's probably it—the meatballs," he says, putting his stethoscope away. "Schnauzers have finicky stomachs."

"But his nose is warm, isn't it?" I'm beginning to feel a little foolish.

"Not really."

"So you think he'll be okay?"

"Probably. Cut down on his food a little—maybe three-quarters the usual portion today. And don't give him any more people food. If he has a recurrence of vomiting or he seems worse, bring him out to the clinic."

"I feel terrible getting you up in the middle of the night. I guess you must think I'm pretty silly."

"No, you're conscientious, the same as you are or your noncanine clients."

"It's more than that. I'm beginning to understand how the Harts feel . . . If anything were to happen to him—"

"He's going to be fine. You're just a little nervous, like most new mothers." He says this with a smile, in a voice not at all condescending, but kind. It's the kindness that makes me cry.

I start toward the kitchen hoping he won't notice the tears. "I made some coffee," I say, but I feel his hand on my shoulder, and when I turn around he kisses me. There's no hesitation in this kiss, no holding back. I don't hold back, either. There's nothing to get in our way except Sherman, who lets out a sharp little yelp when I accidentally step on his foot.

If I wrote a memo to the File of Myself, that longstanding controversy between my head and my heart, it would go something like this:

MEMO TO FILE
SARAH BRIGHT BAYNARD, ATTORNEY, PLAINTIFF
V.
SALLY BAYNARD, WOMAN, DEFENDANT

It has come to my attention that there is an inherent conflict of interest between the Plaintiff and the Defendant. This conflict is of many years duration but recent events have made it impossible to ignore. The parties have reached a crisis in their very close relationship. The Plaintiff (hereinafter Attorney) ignored one of the most basic tenets of professionalism by having sexual relations with a witness in an ongoing case, this taking place in the presence of a third party, one canine whose welfare Attorney is charged with protecting. Plaintiff was fully aware that what she was doing was unethical. Defendant (hereinafter Woman), however, felt nothing of the kind. Without hesitation she invited the witness into her bedroom, closed the door, and proceeded to enjoy herself as she had not done in years. Meanwhile, said canine observed the proceedings from his position on the floor next to the bed. When Woman (attorneys do not make noises like this) began to moan, canine began to bark loudly. Whereupon the witness began to laugh, and this brought about a situation which can only be described as disastrous. Woman's (and Attorney's) elderly mother was awakened, came into the room and, upon observing her daughter and witness naked in the bed and laughing hysterically, began screaming. Witness hurried to clothe himself and left Woman's home in great haste.

To further illustrate the inherent conflict

of interest between Attorney and Woman, it must be noted that on the morning following this incident, Attorney feels terrible and Woman feels better than she has in many years. Were Attorney and Woman not sharing the same body this would not be a problem, but under the circumstances some action must be taken to cure the conflict.

Attorney is presently ethically obligated to act in the best interests of the canine and this obligation must supersede her own desires as Woman. Until such time as Attorney is free from this obligation, Woman must terminate her relationship (if indeed it *is* a relationship) with the witness. She may also wish to think carefully before she attempts to explain this incident to her mother.

In addition to the conflict of interest between Attorney and Woman, there exists a further complication in this matter: Woman has become emotionally attached to the canine whose interests she has been ordered to protect, and this attachment may threaten her ability to render unbiased judgment in the case.

Note: This memo is highly confidential, intended for the parties only, and should be destroyed after reading.

Such a Little Sexpot

At the breakfast table my mother looks more exhausted than usual, but she doesn't seem to remember what happened last night.

"Come on, Mom, try to eat your cereal."

"Can't . . ." she says, her voice weak.

"Can't what?"

"Sw . . . swim."

"You don't have to swim today if you don't want to." She's always liked the indoor condo pool, oblivious to the group of old men who frequent the shallow end. They never swim, they just stand around, waist deep, talking and talking. Delores, always the keen observer, has shared her thoughts on this: *They pee in there, I know it. Old men can't hold it that long!*

"No, I mean . . ." My mother opens her mouth and points down her throat.

"Swallow?"

She nods. "Can't."

"Do you have a sore throat?" She shakes her head. "What about some scrambled eggs and grits? That would be easy to swallow."

She won't eat, but she seems content with Sherman in her lap. She strokes his back as if she's always had a dog to keep her company at the breakfast table.

"He's a good dog, isn't he, Mom?" She smiles. I miss this smile. So often these days she just stares blankly, as if the world has been drained of everything interesting.

When Delores comes she eyes Sherman and says, rather dramatically, "Oh, Lord, *he's* still here," but I can tell she's having a hard time holding onto her disapproval.

Suddenly my mother's smile disappears and she points to me: "Naked!"

"She's really going downhill fast,' I whisper to Delores.

"That's what I've been trying to tell you," Delores mouths back.

My mother's mind sputters and sparks, then fires: "Such a little sexpot," she shouts, her index finger still aimed at me.

"That's not nice, Miz Margaret. You behave yourself now!" says Delores.

I can't get away from the condo fast enough. "Come on, Sherman, we're already late." Sherman jumps down from my mother's lap, follows me to the door, those black eyes full of questions: *Why are you in such a rush? I was just getting used to those ladies, and now you're taking me away? Where's the vet? What am I doing here, anyway?*

"You need this?" says Delores, holding Dr. Borden's hat, a faded Red Sox cap, which he'd left on the table.

"It belongs to a friend," I say on my way out.

"You better be careful out there today," she warns. "It's Friday the thirteenth."

On the drive to the office Sherman sits in the passenger seat, his nose turned toward the window. The radio is full of bad news, so I turn it off.

"You want the window down, honey?" I ask. "I guess it's okay, as long as you don't jump out."

He looks at me with his answer: *Why would I do that? I'm not stupid!*

But the moment I roll the window down he curls his front paws over the door handle and I reach over to grab his collar. His eyes reproach me: *I'm fine. Just want to get a better view. Don't want to miss any smells, either.*

"Sorry. I didn't mean to pull you so hard. We'll be at the office in just a minute. I've got a client coming in, but you can play with Gina. She can be a real pain in the butt sometimes, but she'll be on her best behavior with you because she likes handsome guys."

I don't think he's listening now, but I like talking to him. "I hope we didn't freak you out too much last night, the vet and I."

He turns around at the word "vet": *I don't understand what you're saying, but you seem excited about whatever it is.*

• • •

"You might want to turn your collar up a little," Gina whispers in my ear as I follow Natalie Carter back to my office.

"What?"

"To hide that hickey, or whatever it is."

"Tell her I'll be a minute," I say, ducking into the bathroom. There's a purplish-red blotch on my neck, just below my left ear. I follow Gina's advice; the upturned collar almost covers it.

If Mrs. Carter notices anything she handles it gracefully. "You're looking really nice this morning. New haircut?"

"No, but thanks."

"Something's different—I'm not sure what—but it's a good look."

I open her file. "So, Derwood says he's going to represent himself. I can't force him to hire a lawyer, but it's going to make things more difficult."

"He wants to meet with you before he answers the complaint. He says he wants to 'spare me unnecessary distress.'"

"What does that mean?"

"He knows some things," she says.

Okay, I think, here we go. *Now* she's going to tell me everything she should have told me in our first meeting, before I filed the complaint and had it served on her husband. Hadn't I given her my standard advice? *You need to tell me everything. Think of it this way: I'm your lawyer for everything you tell me, but for everything you* don't *tell me, I'm not your lawyer.*

"What things?"

"I had an affair, but it was years ago. I didn't think he'd have the nerve to bring it up, considering his behavior."

"How long ago?"

"At least five years. It was just a brief fling, but I felt so guilty I told him about it. I shouldn't have."

"Did he forgive you?"

"He said he did, but every now and then, when I'd get mad about his . . . his bedding down with his court reporter . . . he'd bring it up again. We've slept together plenty of times after that, if that matters."

"It matters. Was this the only time you were unfaithful?"

"Yes."

"Natalie, it's essential that you tell me everything."

"That was the only time."

I scan my notes from our first meeting. "After you discovered he was still sleeping with his court reporter, this last time . . . in September . . . you left him, and you haven't slept with him since then, right?"

"That's right." Mrs. Carter opens her purse, retrieves a compact, applies some lip gloss. "They're all jerks, aren't they?"

"Excuse me?"

"Men."

"Not all of them, I guess."

"I mean, they're so used to doing whatever they want, and having us put up with it—they're actually shocked when we finally say, 'Enough!'"

I look at my watch. The watch comes in handy when I need to move things along. "If there's anything else I need to know, please tell me before we go any further."

"No. That's it. I've been a good girl ever since."

"Since Derwood won't hire a lawyer, I'll meet with him, but I doubt it will be productive. I'm going to write him a letter first, for the file, to remind him—as he knows already—that it's not advisable for him to proceed without representation. If he insists on being pro se, I'll ask him to prepare a proposal for settlement."

"That sounds good," she says. "There was something else I wanted to ask you about . . . The furniture I inherited from my mother, and her china . . ." She goes on and on about Queen Anne this and Wedgewood that. I'm having a hard time concentrating. Tony Borden is getting in the way.

It's been a long time for me, he said.

Me, too.

You don't seem like a woman who would spend a lot of time alone. You're so . . . I don't know . . . luscious.

I'm just plain old Sally.

There's nothing plain about you. I've been thinking about this ever since we had dinner.

You have?

I've been thinking, is it possible in a million years that a woman like you would want to get together with a sad old veterinarian?

You're not old. Maybe a little sad.

See, you noticed it already.

Sad is the wrong word. Serious.

Whatever it is, I come with plenty of baggage.

Doesn't everybody?

I guess so. Speaking of which—what about the judge?

Oh, he's got his share.

No, I mean, you and the judge.

It's got nothing to do with you and me.

But it does, if you're still in love with him.

I was confused for a while, but not anymore. Like we were saying, everybody comes with baggage. Even Sherman.

When Natalie Carter's voice yanks me back into the room I apologize. "I feel like I'm coming down with something," I say.

"You look a little flushed," she says.

I can't get his voice out of my head. My heart's still banging against my ribs. It's just a dumb muscle, but it's persistent, and I can feel it trying to pound some sense into my brain.

Another One?

No dogs in the courthouse, Ms. Baynard," says the deputy stationed at the metal detector just inside the entrance.

"He's my client," I say, winking. I know this guy. I come through this detector maybe twenty times a month. "Seriously, I have permission."

"I don't know . . ."

"We have a meeting with Judge Baynard."

Sherman perks his ears as if to say, *Please.* The deputy melts. "I guess he don't look too dangerous."

"He's a sweetheart." I put my briefcase and my keys in the plastic bucket.

"Better take that collar off him before he goes through. That tag will set the system off. Nice little fellow. What kind?"

"Miniature schnauzer."

"You sure this is okay?"

"I'm his court-appointed guardian. We're going to see the judge about his case." All this is true, but it's hard for me to keep a straight face.

"Okay, but keep him on the leash."

"Yes, sir."

There's a crowd waiting for the elevator so Sherman and I take the stairs to the second floor. He's in heaven on the staircase—so many new smells, the delicious deposits from so many shoes, odors from all over Charleston County and beyond. He pauses every other step or so, his nose trembling, his docked tail twitching with excitement. "Come on, boy," I say, trying not to tug the leash too hard, but in the stairwell he finds a treasure, a McDonald's bag still giving off the scent of hamburger. "No, honey, leave that alone. It'll make you sick."

From behind her desk outside Joe Baynard's chambers, his secretary, Betty, can see us coming down the hall.

"Is the judge busy?" I ask.

"Who's this?"

"This is Sherman, the star of *Hart v. Hart*. Sherman, say hello to Betty."

"I see why they're fighting over him. How'd you get him in here?"

"He charmed his way in. Anybody with the judge?"

"He's working on an order, but I'll tell him you're here."

"Thanks."

She buzzes her boss. "Sally Baynard's here . . . No . . . I didn't ask her . . ." She turns to me. "What's this about?"

"My motion to bifurcate in the Hart case." I say this loud enough for him to hear through Betty's receiver. "And some related matters."

"It'll be a few minutes," says Betty.

"I'll wait." Sherman sits on my lap, content to let me rub him under the chin.

"Looks like you've got a new boyfriend," Betty says.

I wait ten minutes. "Would you remind him I'm out here?"

She knocks on the door to his chambers, steps inside. There's some conversation, then she comes out. "He doesn't think it's advisable for you to discuss the Hart case with him unless the other two lawyers are present. And he said to remind you that you can submit a supporting brief for your motion."

"No," I say firmly, "I'm not going to wait any longer." I walk right past Betty, fling open the door.

"What do you think you're doing, barging in like this?" My ex-husband pushes the desk drawer closed, the one where he keeps his stash of fingernails. I let Sherman off the leash. He's happy to have new territory to investigate. He disappears under the desk, comes out with one of Joe's shoes.

"Give me that!" Joe shouts.

I've practiced my speech on the way to the courthouse. It's short, to the point: "I know I'm violating the rules of professional conduct by coming over here to talk to you without notifying the other lawyers in the case, but you've forced me into it. You have two choices: (1) grant my motion, because you have no good reason to deny it, or (2) refuse to schedule the motion, and I'll report you to the judicial ethics committee."

But then I can't stop. "And when I make my report I'll tell the committee what's REALLY going on here: you appointed me as guardian ad litem for this dog, not because you want someone to protect his interests or even someone to settle the case, but because you have the crazy idea that you're still in love with me." I try to control my voice, but I hear myself shouting. Sherman crawls back under Joe's desk.

"I didn't file the case, Sally," he says, "so I don't know how you can think—Would you please take my shoe away from him before he—"

"You didn't have the guts to be up front with me, to say, *Sally, I'm still in love with you,* so you involved me in a case that's likely to go on forever, because these people will never settle, and you'll have the pleasure of having me captive in your courtroom for a dozen motion hearings and then a trial that will take—what would you say—two weeks, three, a month?"

"Sally—"

"And then when you found out that the vet and I had . . . that we'd been to dinner together . . . you got jealous, decided you'd punish me with that ridiculous order giving me temporary custody of Sherman. But you know what? I like having him around!"

"If you don't calm down I'm going to have to call a deputy," he says.

"Fine. Throw me in the lockup. I don't care, but the dog will have to go with me."

"Okay," he says, "I admit it wasn't good judgment, the way I've handled this Hart case, but I'll grant your motion, and we'll get the dog part of the case over with, let things settle down, and then you and I—"

"Stop it, Joe!"

"I know you still feel something for me. We've never really let go of each other." Before I know it he has his arms around me. "Don't deny it."

"Please stop." He still smells the same, feels the same.

"You've never thought about getting back together?"

I pull myself away from him. "That's irrelevant."

"The rules of evidence don't apply here, Sally. You want *me* to be honest. What about you?"

"Of course I still care about you, but—"

"You're not answering the question: Haven't you thought about us giving it another try?"

"Why would anything be different?"

"Because we're both a lot wiser."

This makes me laugh. Sherman emerges from under the desk with the shoe. "Is *this* wise? What you're doing right now? What about Susan?"

"Susan doesn't care."

"I don't believe that. Have you been to counseling?"

"No, it wouldn't do any good."

"You have to try."

"It's that vet, isn't it?" We stand nose to nose. "Come on, answer me."

"Joe, when you can tell me you and Susan have been to counseling—and I don't mean some token visit—then maybe we can continue this conversation. Come on, Sherman, let's go."

"Who's on the schedule this afternoon?" I ask Gina when I get back.

"Rick Silber. Harold Duncan, to prepare for his deposition. Some college student who wants to intern next summer."

"I don't even know if I want an intern this summer. Ask her—"

"Him."

"Ask him to call back in May."

"Want to hear something funny? Last time Rick came in, he asked me if I thought he was attractive."

"Wow, that was direct."

"But it wasn't like he was making a pass or anything. He said he just wanted my honest opinion."

"And?"

"I told him he'd be more attractive if he got rid of the goatee and stopped wearing socks with his sandals."

"You didn't."

"I did. Come to think of it, I should have told him to get himself a regular pair of shoes. Oh . . . I almost forgot to tell you. His wife dropped her counterclaim. Her lawyer sent the dismissal order this morning."

"So, Rick should be happy. Have you let him know?"

"I thought you'd want to tell him yourself. Oh, and about the Harts. You asked me to call them and set up some times for them to visit with Sherman."

"Not together. Separately."

"Right. I can't reach either one of them, but I'll keep trying."

When Rick Silber comes in he kicks off his sandals, revealing—no socks this time—his tiny, tender-looking feet. He assumes his usual lotus position on my sofa. Sherman sniffs around the sandals, but rejects them. "I don't like dogs," Rick says. "It's kind of irrational, but—"

"He doesn't bite. Sherman, come over here, honey. Good news, Rick. Your wife dropped the counterclaim. It's over."

"She's always been the one who controls everything."

I can't believe this. I take a deep breath. "Let's go back to the beginning of the case. You left Debra, moved in with your graduate student, and after a year of separation you filed for divorce. Your wife counterclaimed adultery, we were gearing up for a big battle, and then she got cancer. Then your graduate student left you, you told me you didn't want to go through with the divorce, but I explained that we still had to defend against the counterclaim. And you were miserable, right?"

"Right." This is about the time he'd start to pull at his goatee, but the goatee is gone.

"So now, for whatever reason, Debra decides to drop the counterclaim, and you're still unhappy."

"I know, I'm screwed up."

"Rick, the case is over now. There's really nothing more I can do."

"I know, I think that's why I'm so . . . I don't know . . . I'm going to miss talking to you and Gina."

"Last time we talked you complained about my fees . . . like I was making up work so I could charge you for it."

"You know I didn't mean it. You've been very patient. And Gina's been really great, too."

"I'll pass that along to her."

"I don't mind paying if I can . . . you know . . . if I can keep coming in every now and then."

"Rick, your case is over. Now if you ever decide you want to go ahead with a divorce—"

"No. That's probably why she dropped the

counterclaim. Her cancer's the really aggressive kind. She probably won't last six months."

"I'm sorry to hear that."

"Yes. The whole thing just makes me feel like a total jerk."

"You're going through a difficult time."

"It's my wife who's going through hell. Do you think, now that this legal stuff is over, I should call her, apologize?"

"I don't know your wife, how she'd react."

"But you're so . . . You always seem to know how to handle everything."

"If you knew what's been happening in my life lately, you wouldn't say that."

"I don't know why that makes me feel better, but it does," Rick says.

Dog King of the World

When I walk into the kitchen with Sherman, Delores scowls. "Well, if it isn't the Dog King of the World. Fancy as he is, he ought to know better than to leave his calling card on the carpet."

"What?"

"Back in your bedroom, in the corner by the dresser. You didn't see it this morning?"

"No, of course not. I wouldn't have left it for you to clean up."

"I *didn't* clean it up. I don't do dog poop." She lifts her eyelids extra high so I'll know she's mad. "If you got a boyfriend, I don't know why you have to keep his dog."

"The dog doesn't belong to him." I feel my face getting hot. "Anyway, this is my private life."

"It's not private when your mama wakes up from her nap this afternoon hollering about some man in your bedroom. I said, 'You calm down, Miz Margaret, there's no man in that bedroom.' I took her in there to see for herself, but she kept hollering. Her mind's a mess, but this isn't in her mind!"

"It won't happen again."

"You do what you want to do with your love life and all, but just remember she's a sick woman.

You need to find a place for her, but it seems like you got other things on your mind."

"I looked at that one place. I have two others to see. How's Charlie?"

"Feeling real puny. His sister's helping out, but he'll do better when I'm with him full time."

"I hear you, Delores. I do."

"Sit down and relax a minute before I go." Her voice softens. "I was just heating up your mama's supper. Right, honey?" My mother smiles weakly. Sherman has finished his peregrinations around the condo and comes back to the kitchen. "You! You sit down, too!" Delores commands, but my mother reaches for him and he lifts his front paws to her knees, begging to be held. "All right, honey," she says to my mother, "you can hold him until supper's ready."

While my mother is preoccupied with Sherman, I motion for Delores to join me in the living room.

"Delores, you wouldn't put Charlie in a nursing home, would you?"

"No, but I'm in a different place in my life than you are. When I finish here, Charlie's going to be my whole life. I'm done raising my children, done with everything else except this one thing. So I'm ready."

"I wish I were more like you."

"And maybe I wish I was more like *you—*

smart and sassy, a lawyer and all, no money problems, all that—but we are who we are."

"I'll miss you, Delores. And *she'll* miss you." I look over at my mother, who seems perfectly content with Sherman in her lap. "I know I haven't been very sensitive about your situation with Charlie."

"I'll tend to that. You tend to this situation here. And don't forget the situation back in your bedroom." She laughs when she sees my confusion. "I mean that pile of you-know-what over by the closet. It's getting pretty ripe, lying there all day. Even Dog King of the World's got stinky poop."

When she first moved in with me, after the Alzheimer's diagnosis, my mother would follow me around the kitchen, looking over my shoulder, making suggestions—*I think you might want a little more salt in that. If you leave that in the oven too long, it's going to dry out*—until I wanted to scream. But lately she's lost interest in food. I sit across from her, coax her. "Try to finish that, Mom."

She nods, her mouth full of mashed potatoes, then spits them out, mostly onto the plate but some onto her blouse. "Mess," she says.

"Mess is right, but don't worry, we need to wash this blouse anyway. What about some meatloaf?"

"No," she says, and points to her sweatpants. "Mess."

Now I smell it. "Okay, we'll deal with it." I help her back to her bathroom, Sherman following close behind. My mother holds onto the back of the toilet as I remove her soiled pants and underpants, wipe her bottom, then unbutton her blouse. Sherman buries his nose in the pile of clothes on the floor. "Stop it, Sherman!" I yell. He backs off, chastened, and sits obediently while I shower her off and help her into a fresh diaper. It makes me sad to see how she tolerates this indignity. She's always taken such pride in her pretty underwear, those satiny, lacy things that now lie unused in the drawer. When I open it to get a clean undershirt—she's given up bras, too—there's the scent of lavender sachets. Once I would have thought those sachets were silly. Now I miss the mother who put them there.

I get her settled in bed and Sherman hops up beside her, licks her face, then nestles on the end of the bed, between her feet. She's calmer with him nearby, content. "I bet you'd like to keep him, wouldn't you, Mom?" I say, and she nods, but I realize it's cruel to involve her in my fantasy. "Want a story?" No, she's too sleepy.

I leave the door open a crack, go back to the refrigerator to scrounge for something, but nothing appeals. This is one of those nights when the silence doesn't soothe; it stirs up all my worries. What am I going to do with my mother? How will I tell her I'm putting her in a nursing home? Will she even understand what I'm saying, and if she doesn't, is that a blessing?

And what's going to happen to Sherman? It's an absurd idea, impossible, but I imagine myself on the witness stand: *Your honor, I've concluded my investigation. While I'm convinced that both Mr. and Mrs. Hart are fully capable of caring for Sherman, I'm also convinced that if you choose between the two of them, the dispute will never end. I'm not a psychologist, yet it's clear to me that the fight over Sherman isn't about what's best for him, but about what's broken in the Harts' marriage. How will they ever work together in Sherman's best interest? I could recommend that you award custody to Mrs. Hart and give Mr. Hart visitation with Sherman, or vice versa, but this would only involve the dog in their continuing bitterness. Look how many motions they've filed, many of them concerning the dog. There will never be a "final order" in this case. They won't ever stop. The only solution is to give him to a neutral third party.*

And in my fantasy, my ex-husband looks down from the bench at me, comes to his senses enough to say, *What about you, Ms. Baynard?*

And then the fantasy gets even better. Tony Borden, who's sitting at the back of the courtroom, stands: *Your honor, as you know, I've been involved with Sherman his whole life, almost five years now. I've come to know both Mr. and Mrs. Hart very well, and although I believe that they are each fully capable of giving Sherman a good home and meeting his needs, I agree with Ms. Baynard's assessment. I believe your idea is the perfect solution to a difficult situation. If you decide to allow Ms. Baynard to keep Sherman, I will of course do whatever I can to assist her.*

"Don't be ridiculous, Sally!" I hear myself saying. Am I losing my mind, like my mother?

I try some TV for a while, CNN. Trouble in Afghanistan, Pakistan. Shootings in Chicago. The stock market up.

My own stockbroker left a message a couple of weeks ago but I haven't had time to call him back. I know what he's going to say, *You might want to think about being a little less conservative with your investments.* Maybe I'm too cautious with my meager nest egg, but I can't afford to lose any of it. If I have to raid my retirement account to pay for a nursing home, I'll be the Dowager of Domestic Relations until I drop. I turn off the TV, rummage through a stack of magazines for something soothing, but everything seems either too real (home-grown terrorists, global warming, the coming water shortage) or too unreal (mother-daughter bonding through cosmetic surgery). Maybe, I think, the real and the unreal are merging in some cosmic screwup, and I'm right in the middle of it.

I call my friend Ellen. "I'm sorry I woke you up."

"I just dozed off. Terrible day in court," she says.

"What happened?"

"Mistrial. Defense lawyer was drunk."

"Not somebody from the P.D.'s office, I hope."

"No. That young guy from the Holz firm. He was acting weird during his opening argument, wobbling over to the jury box, slurring, then he fell asleep after I called my first witness."

"I thought he'd gone to rehab."

"Guess it didn't take. His wife will probably be calling you any time now. Anyway, what's up?"

I tell her about my meeting with Joe. "I feel terrible about it."

"Sounds like you handled it well."

"I think he felt rejected."

"That's the way he *should* feel."

"I know, but he really needs a good friend right now."

"Right. It just can't be you. You know that— that's why you told him you wouldn't talk again until he's been through counseling. By then you'll be out of the dog case."

"He could still deny my motion."

"I don't think he's *that* irrational. He'll grant it, he'll schedule a short trial on the dog-custody issue, and that'll be it. You'll feel a lot better when this case is over."

"I guess so."

"You don't sound so sure."

"I'll miss the dog."

"So get a dog."

"But it won't be Sherman."

"You've really fallen for that little guy, haven't you?"

"When he looks at me with those eyes, it's like he knows how I'm feeling."

"Maybe he does."

"But he's just a *dog*. I never imagined—"

"What? You never imagined you could love an animal this much?"

"I don't exactly *love* him."

"What would you call it, then? There's nothing wrong with loving the dog. He probably feels the same way about you by now."

"Maybe."

"What else is going on?" Ellen presses. "You sound terrible."

"Delores is leaving. Charlie's sick."

"Oh, God."

"I've got to find a nursing home. I went to one of those places in Mt. Pleasant. It was okay, but I just can't imagine putting her there."

"Wendy Shuler's father has Alzheimer's. He's

in a nursing home. Wendy says it's pretty good. Compassionate Care."

"That one's on my list. I just haven't had time . . ."

"Why don't you go tomorrow? I'll watch your mother."

"That's no way for you to spend your Saturday."

"I'll bring some work over," she says. "Hank's playing golf."

"You're wonderful, Ellen."

"We do these things for each other, right? Remember when I went into labor with Mandy? It was three in the morning, Hank was out of town. You came right over, drove me to the hospital?"

"Yeah, you were screaming all the way down Calhoun Street for me to go faster, and then when I hit the accelerator you screamed for me to slow down."

"Anything else going on? Besides your mother?"

I give her a detailed report about my night with the vet. "Not exactly a great start to a relationship, is it?"

"If you can't see the humor in that situation, you're worse off than I thought."

"It was awful."

"What, the sex?"

"No, *that* was great, but I should never have let . . . Mom was so upset."

"Have you talked to him?"

"No, I've been waiting for him to call."

"This isn't high school. Why don't you call him?"

"I'm afraid to."

"What are you afraid of?"

"He'll be polite, but who wants to get involved with a woman who's living with her demented mother?"

"You're going to put her in a home, right?"

"I guess so."

"Are you crying?"

"No."

"You are," she says emphatically.

"I'm losing it, with all this stuff going on at once."

"It's going to work out. You'll find a decent place for your mother, and you and the vet— What's that noise?" Ellen asks.

"The dog. I think he needs to go out."

"Wow, he sounds desperate. I'll be there tomorrow by ten, okay?"

Sherman is desperate, all right, but not because he has to pee. When I open the front door he refuses to follow me, barks even louder, turns back down the hall and into my mother's bedroom. She's not in her bed, but on the bathroom floor beside the toilet, the diaper around her feet. She's not hurt, thank goodness. I lift her up—it's amazing how heavy she is, though she's lost weight—and onto the toilet. When she's finished I help her back to bed.

"Good dog," I say as Sherman hops up beside her. I sit for a while in the easy chair nearby to make sure she's okay. Sherman's vigilant, too. Only when he hears her snoring does his head nestle into the bedspread. In the dim glow of the night-light I watch until he falls asleep, his chest rising and falling, his legs chasing something only Dog King of the World, in his dreams, can see.

Trying Dogfully

There's no "marketing director" here, just a director who doesn't seem to care that I don't have an appointment. He takes me on the tour himself. "All of our rooms have windows onto the community garden," he explains. "Mildred and Tallie are planting bulbs for the spring." Two old ladies sit on the edge of one of the raised beds, working the dirt with trowels. "We encourage all our residents who're physically able to adopt a small area as their own."

We pass a room with a piano and a circle of chairs. "A volunteer from the college music department comes once a week to lead a song session," he says. "Even the residents who can't sing enjoy listening. And afterward we have an ice-cream social."

"My mother would like that," I say.

"We also work with a local high school. Their kids partner with our residents—read to them, walk with them around the grounds, work in the garden. Most of the kids don't have grandparents close by, so they get as much out of it as our residents do."

When the director opens the door into the courtyard, a big dog with a coat the color of caramel, approaches us. "Say hello to Ms. Baynard, Sadie." The dog sits, lifts her paw. "Sadie's a rescue dog."

"So you allow pets?" I ask.

"Just this one. She lives here. She's welcome in all the common areas. Official policy is that she's not supposed to go into individual rooms, but, as you can imagine, there's a good deal of cheating. Sadie's our most popular resident. Lots of admirers . . . and they keep her well-groomed, as you can see."

We finish our tour. "Don't hesitate to call me if you have any more questions," he says. "This is always a difficult decision."

As I drive away, I realize this is as good as it's going to get. I'm running out of time and I'm not going to find a better place. Delores needs to be with Charlie. But when I imagine leaving my mother here—no matter how compassionate the care—I break into a sweat.

Sure, I'll visit every day. And maybe she won't remember that I promised her I'd never put her in a nursing home. Maybe she won't even know where she is.

But *I'll* know.

When I get back to the condo Ellen and my mother are sitting on the sofa looking through a magazine, Sherman at their feet. "Margaret and I have been having fun," Ellen says. "We were thinking maybe it would be nice for her to try a new hairdo, something shorter, maybe something like this." It's true, my mother's once perfectly coiffed silver hair hangs limp and thin, almost to her shoulders. Until the last couple of weeks Delores and I have been able to help her put it up into her customary chignon, but now she pulls out the bobby pins before we're halfway done. "See, isn't this one pretty?" My mother smiles. "How'd it go? The place, I mean."

"Much better than the other one. Thanks so much for doing this, Ellen."

"My pleasure. By the way, the vet called. He said he tried your cell but you didn't pick up. Want to call him back while I'm here?"

"No."

"Okay, fine, be that way. But you're going to have to give me all the details sooner or later."

My mother needs a nap, so I settle her in bed and read aloud from *Travels with Charley*. She's soothed by the sound of my voice, the familiarity of the story of Steinbeck's cross-country trip with his dog. She doesn't notice when I flip back and forth looking for my favorite passages.

Once Charley fell in love with a dachshund, a romance racially unsuitable, physically ridiculous, and mechanically impossible. But all these problems Charley ignored. He loved deeply and tried dogfully.

I am happy to report that in the war between reality and romance, reality is not the stronger.

I used to have a sense of humor about my life. I could laugh at myself, laugh about all the relationships that had failed, talk to my girlfriends in that self-deprecating way that probably never fooled them. I was so confident, so sure that if I ever really wanted to settle down with a man, I would find the right one, and equally sure that I could be happy all by myself. But something's changed.

Once my mother's asleep I call the vet. He's at home. I've rehearsed a smooth way into the conversation, something about how grateful I am that when I called about Sherman, he didn't hesitate. "You came right away."

He laughs. "Maybe too quick?"

"That's not what I meant."

"Be honest."

"It was fine. Better than fine. You left your hat here, by the way."

"How's Sherman?"

"No more stomach problems. He seems to be settling right in."

"I told you you'd like having a dog around. Carmen's still available when you're ready."

"Carmen?"

"The beagle who needs a good home."

"Well, I've got my hands full right now with Sherman."

"Maryann and Rusty must be going nuts without him," he says.

"They both visited with him Thursday— separately, of course. But we didn't hear from them all day yesterday."

"Would you like to go to dinner tonight?" he asks.

"I've got my mother."

"I could bring something over. Maybe something from the seafood place."

"That's really sweet, but I think I'd better let my mother have a quiet night." Right away, I worry that he's going to take this the wrong way, so I try again. "I'd love to go to dinner. I just wish things weren't so complicated right now."

"What's so complicated?"

"My mother, I guess."

"Lots of people have mothers," he says.

"She's not doing well at all, and the woman who stays with her during the day will be leaving soon, so I need to find a nursing home. Maybe once she's settled somewhere, I'll have more free time."

"You're not the only one whose life is complicated. I have my son. He lives with his mother in San Francisco."

"How old is he?"

"Twelve."

"That must be hard for you, to have him so far away."

"He's the one who suffers the most."

"Do you think dogs suffer like we do?"

"They suffer, but not in the same ways. Sherman, for example, isn't plagued by self-doubt. He misses Maryann and Rusty, and their disappearance is a mystery to him, but he isn't worried that he did something wrong. He'll allow himself to be comforted. He'll accept your love without worrying about whether he deserves it."

After the call, I tell myself I should try being more like Sherman.

Off the Deep End

Michelle Marvel just called," Gina says when I get to the office on Monday morning. "Mr. Hart is in the hospital. She said it's all Mrs. Hart's fault."

"Oh, for God's sake."

"He had a heart attack on Friday, when he went to get Mrs. Hart out of jail!"

"Slow down, you're not making any sense."

"That's why we couldn't reach either one of them. She was arrested on Thursday night, and he had the heart attack on Friday when he went to get her out."

"Arrested for what?"

"Burglary."

"That can't be right."

"I know, it doesn't sound right, but Michelle was sure about it. She wanted me to let you know that Mr. Hart would like to see you as soon as possible. He's at Roper, cardiac intensive care, second floor."

"He's not *dying,* is he?"

"She didn't know the details, just that he's in intensive care."

"What about his wife?"

"He posted bond for her, got her out of jail, was

driving her home when he had the heart thing."

"You really think it's an emergency? I was planning to work on the brief in support of the motion for bifurcation."

"I've already done the research, I can draft it," Gina says. "Come on, the old guy's had a heart attack. He's asking for you."

I think about the old man at Golden Memories, Mr. Charles Bird in his striped pajamas. "You're right, I'll go."

"No visitors allowed yet," says the nurse at the nurses' station, "except close family."

"I'm his lawyer." Not exactly true, but close enough. "He asked to see me."

"Try to keep it under fifteen minutes. Room 205, end of the hall."

Rusty Hart's eyes are closed when I enter the room. He's a big man, but all the machines with their wires and tubes and blinking lights have reduced him to a smaller version of himself. One arm rests on his belly, the other is trapped by an IV taped to the inside of his elbow. The movement of his heartbeat across the monitor seems erratic, distressed.

I decide not to wake him, but the aide who comes with the dinner tray doesn't hesitate. "Sir, let's try to sit you up. Maybe your daughter would like to help you eat?" Mr. Hart's eyes open, searching the room. He yanks the tubing out of his nose. The orderly reinserts it. "No, sir, you don't need to take that out to eat. It's your oxygen." Mr. Hart growls. The orderly vanishes.

I lift the plastic cover off the tray: watery bouillon, plastic cup of apple juice, orange jello. "Here, let me help you."

"Anna?"

"No, Mr. Hart, it's Sally Baynard. You wanted me—"

"Right."

"Would you like some soup?" I pick up the spoon. He pushes it away.

"Feel terrible."

"I know you do. Maybe we should talk later, when you feel better."

"No. Need you to take care of some things . . ." He's very pale, all that ruddiness gone.

"I assume you have a will, Mr. Hart. If you need to update it, I'm sure Michelle Marvel can—"

"Not the will. Shit, if I . . . croak . . . I guess she . . . Maryann . . . should have it all anyway. What the hell. Sherman . . ."

"Sherman's at my house. He's fine for now."

"My buddy."

"They won't let me stay long. What can I do for you?"

"Call Anna."

"I'll ask Michelle to do that, okay?"

"She doesn't know about Anna." I'm stunned he didn't tell his own lawyer about his daughter. "Please."

"What do you want me to tell her?"

"Whatever you think is . . . best."

"I shouldn't be the one deciding what's best for your family."

"You couldn't screw it up more than it is already. You still have the number?"

"I think so."

"Look in my wallet . . ." He points to the little closet across from the bed. "Number's in there, under the picture." And there it is, on a piece of paper tucked behind a small photo. Anna must have been six or seven, missing some front teeth, her reluctant smile coaxed by the school photographer. "Tell her that her mother's gone off the deep end," he says. "*Arrested,* for God's sake." The wavy green line on the monitor behind him spikes sharply up.

"Mr. Hart, this is upsetting you."

"Damn right it's upsetting."

"We can talk later."

"Can you believe it? Burglary!"

"But that can't be right—"

"They broke into a house . . . Cut though a screened porch with box cutters . . . to rescue some dog they said was . . . abused."

"Who's 'they'?"

"Maryann and some other women. Some group

she belongs to. Bunch of crazies. Lucky she didn't get shot."

"You put up her bail?"

"What the hell else was I . . . supposed to do? She's paid that creep Swinton a small fortune, but she won't call him when she gets arrested! She'd still be in jail if my old buddy the magistrate hadn't called me . . ."

"You're a good husband."

"No, just a fixer."

I stand up. "I'll call your daughter. You get some rest."

"Off the deep end, I tell you."

His eyes are closed again, his voice almost inaudible: "You tell my best buddy I miss him. I miss him like hell."

Back at the nurses' station I ask for his nurse. "She's with another patient," says the woman behind the desk, who's busy typing into a computer. "Can I help you?"

"He didn't want his dinner. Someone should check on him."

"Not unusual," she says. "Loss of appetite after a major coronary event. But I'll check on him as soon as I—excuse me, I have a call."

I mouth a "thank you" and leave, wondering if it would have made any difference if I'd said, *He's a sick, lonely old man. His wife's divorcing him, and his daughter probably won't care that he's all alone here. His best buddy is a dog,*

278

and you won't allow dogs in the hospital. So please, he needs some extra attention from you, okay?

When I get back to the office Sherman is sleeping under Gina's desk. "How's Mr. Hart?" she asks.

"Terrible."

"His wife called right after you left. I told her Sherman's doing fine with us. I don't think that's what she wanted to hear."

The call to Anna doesn't go well.

"It's about your father."

"I made it clear I didn't want to get involved."

"He's had a heart attack."

Long pause, as if she's marshaling her defenses. "I'm sorry to hear that."

"He's not doing well at all."

"I'm sure my mother has the situation under control," she says, in that cool, practiced voice.

"They're in the middle of a divorce, remember?"

"So, I get it, you want *me* to drop everything, fly down there, and—"

"Your father is alone in the hospital in very serious condition, and he asked me to let you know." What I'd like to say is, *I don't care how tough your adolescence was, or how much you blame your parents. Your father needs you now.*

"I'll give him a call. What hospital?"

"Roper. Room 205."

"I hope you understand my situation. I work full-time. I have a five-year-old. I have no relationship with my parents."

"Apparently your dad thinks he has one with you."

"He has a hard time with reality."

"He seems pretty grounded to me."

"He's not your father."

"My father died of a heart attack when I was twelve."

"Is that supposed to make me feel guilty?"

"I'm not trying to make you feel anything at all. But he asked me to tell you that your mother's in trouble, too."

"Like what?"

"Like she's been arrested for burglary."

"Very funny."

"I'm just passing this information along, as your father requested. He asked me to tell you she's gone off the deep end. His words, not mine."

"Well, should I thank you for calling?" Her sarcasm could cut through steel. I'm about to hang up when she softens. "Look, I'm sorry."

"I'm sorry, too." And I am. For all of them, for all of *us*.

I rest my head on my desk, something I haven't done since my sleep-deprived college days. It's pleasant, drifting like this, away from everything difficult, but then Gina interrupts.

"Mrs. Hart's here. I told her you were busy. She's visiting with Sherman."

I snap myself back into the case of *Hart v. Hart*. "It's okay. I'll talk to her."

"We had to do it," Mrs. Hart says before I've even asked a question. She's holding Sherman. He burrows his head in the crook of her arm, as if he's rediscovered a secret, special place. I can't help feeling a little jealous.

"Burglary is a felony, Mrs. Hart."

"We didn't actually break into the house, just the screened porch. We had to cut through the screen to get to the dog. A cocker spaniel, poor thing. She was tied up on such a short rope, almost choking to death, half-starved."

"Why didn't you call the police?"

"Sometimes they don't act fast enough, and they'd have taken her to the county shelter. Have you ever been to the shelter?"

"No."

"They do the best they can, but they're always having to cope with budget shortfalls. There are so many animals there! So we—the ARC— we operate independently."

"What's the ARC?"

"Animal Rescue Committee," she says.

"I never heard of it."

"It's just a small local group. I'm the president."

"Were you going to keep the dog?"

"Melanie—she and I are the Sullivan's Island team—would have taken her home, nursed the poor thing back to health, then we'd put out the word on our underground network. Eventually we'd have found a good home for her."

"Have you spoken to your lawyer about this?" I love the thought of Henry Swinton, who only does rich people's divorces, having to dirty his hands in criminal court.

"He's referring me to someone else in his firm, but I've told him I can't afford to pay another legal fee. This is all a big misunderstanding. I'm not a burglar. We didn't intend to do any harm."

"How did you cut the screen?"

"With wire cutters," she says. "We assessed the situation beforehand. Is it burglary if I didn't even go inside the house?"

"Mrs. Hart, I can't advise you on this. All I can tell you is that you'd better take it seriously."

"It's the only thing I've ever done—on my own—that I'm really proud of. I'm not going to apologize for it, but I hope you won't hold it against me in the case with Sherman, because I couldn't bear to lose him. By the way, he doesn't look well. Has he lost weight?"

"He's fine. Dr. Borden saw him recently, so you shouldn't worry."

"Good, because I couldn't bear to think . . ."

"Mrs. Hart, how many dogs have you rescued?"

"This would have been the tenth."

"Did your husband know anything about this?"

"I joined the group after we separated. He wouldn't have approved."

"But he posted bail for you, right?"

She frowns. "I should have called Henry Swinton."

"Why didn't you?"

"I told you, it was all just a big misunderstanding. I thought if I just talked to the magistrate, I could . . . He's a friend of ours. I was sure he'd just let me go, but then the magistrate called Rusty without even asking me. I'd never have—Rusty has such a temper. Once he had me in the car he started yelling. I'm sure that's what brought on the heart attack."

"I guess he had a right to be upset."

"And I guess he's going to blame me for the heart attack."

"He's too sick to do much blaming."

"You don't think he's going to . . ." I can see the fear in her eyes.

"He's very weak, Mrs. Hart."

"Perhaps I should speak to him?"

"I'm sure the lawyers could work something out if you want to talk to him."

"They don't seem to be able to work out *anything*. The whole case has gotten out of control. I wish . . . we could just go back to . . ." She reaches for a tissue.

Gina knocks on the door. "You have that conference call in three minutes," she says.

Mrs. Hart shakes my hand. "Thank you for taking care of Sherman." There's not even a hint of bitterness in her voice. "I'd like to stop by again tomorrow to see him, if that's all right."

Once she's gone Gina says, "There's no conference call, but Ellen's holding for you."

I fill in Ellen on the latest developments. "If the old man dies," she says, "then the case is over. No more hassle with *Hart v. Hart*."

"That's a horrible thing to say."

"Don't tell me you haven't thought about it. If he dies, she'll get the dog. And if you're lonely, you can get a dog of your own. Now, let's talk about tomorrow."

"Tomorrow?"

"Tomorrow is your fiftieth birthday."

"I'd completely forgotten."

"You're taking the day off."

"I don't think so."

"You are, because I called two months ago and asked Gina to mark it off. Maybe you'll do something special for yourself, a massage or a facial or something."

"I've never had a massage or a facial."

"It's not a sin to indulge yourself once in a while, you know. And I've already arranged for Mandy to stay with your mother while we take you out to dinner."

"We?"

"Wendy and Valerie, and Helen, if she doesn't have to babysit the grandchildren. So think about where you want to go."

"I love you, Ellen." I couldn't ask for a better friend, and I'm grateful, but when I hang up, I still feel terrible. "Fifty," I whisper to the empty office. Forty-nine hadn't bothered me, but fifty? What do I have to show for my life? My girl-friends have somehow managed both lawyering and mothering. Wendy Shuler has two sons, grown now, one already out of law school, married with kids. She has three grandchildren. Valerie Onofrio's about to celebrate her twenty-fifth wedding anniversary. Ellen has Hank and Mandy. They all have dogs.

I have my mother—my only child—and I'm about to put her in a nursing home.

Fifty

Of course my mother doesn't remember it's my birthday, but Delores does. She brings a lemon pound cake, my favorite, and lights five candles at the breakfast table. "Five is plenty," she laughs. "Don't want to burn the house down!"

My mother claps, delighted with this little party. She thinks she's the guest of honor. I let her blow out the candles and open my present from Delores: a lacy white nightgown, not the kind of thing I ever wear.

"Thank you, Delores. It's beautiful," I say. "I'll save it for a special occasion."

"Don't be saving it too long. No use in having nice things if you don't use 'em." She winks. "Your mama and me, we want you to be happy. Right, Miz Margaret?"

My mother nods, then turns to me and says, "Ice cream!" I'm delighted she can still make the connection between cake and ice cream. There's some frozen yogurt in the freezer. It's nine in the morning, but why not? I add some swirls of chocolate syrup. My mother takes a big spoonful from her bowl and gets chocolate all over her mouth. Sherman's excited, too. He nudges my calf, letting me know he wants to be held. I lift him into my lap and of course he's immediately interested in the birthday feast.

"Sorry," I say. "I wish you could have some, but it's against doctor's orders."

"I don't think he even knows he's not one of *us*," says Delores. "He thinks he's a member of the family."

"Well, Sherman's sort of like our foster child, aren't you, sweetie? It's going to be hard to give you back."

"Look at his eyes," she says. "It's like he's listening to everything."

"He probably is, but he doesn't understand what we're saying."

"Don't be so sure about that," says Delores. When she clears the table Sherman lets out a little sigh, lowers his head into my lap.

"How's Charlie?" I ask.

"Weak as a kitten, after the chemo."

"He'll feel better when you're with him full-time."

She nods. "So, how're you going to spend your birthday?"

"I'll check on things at the office—unless you'd like to take the rest of the day off."

"No, thanks. I brought us a special movie to watch. *Philadelphia*. About that fellow with AIDS and his lawyer."

"You think Mom can follow it?"

"Maybe not, but she likes Denzel Washington."

"She does?"

"She told me she wants to marry him. Got pretty good taste in men, don't you think?"

"You're hopeless!" says Gina when I show up at the office.

"I'm so far behind."

"But I cleared your calendar for today and tomorrow."

"Why tomorrow?"

"Because I had a hunch you'd come in today, and the only way I'd be able to convince you to leave is if you knew you had tomorrow to catch up. So get out of here. You only turn fifty once."

"Thank God."

"What are you talking about? You look great, though I've been meaning to tell you—don't get mad—I think you could use some color in your hair."

"I don't mind a little gray."

"Just don't let it get out of control. Speaking of which," she says, handing me an envelope. It's a gift certificate to a downtown salon. "They do great work. Maybe they could even fit you in this afternoon . . . And here's something I picked up at the bookstore. Thought it might come in handy in the dog case: *Inside the Canine Mind*."

"Thanks, Gina."

"By the way, Maria Lopez—the secretary over at probate court—called this morning, wanted to know if you'd be interested in representing a cat."

"You're joking."

"Apparently the word's getting around that you do a good job representing animals. Anyway, some old woman on Edisto Island died and left her cat an estate worth millions. In trust, like Leona Helmsley."

"So what do they need me for?"

"She pretty much cut her son out of the will, and he's contesting it. And even if she was in her right mind when she signed the will, she left all these complicated instructions about who should take care of the cat. Interesting, huh? And there's plenty of money to pay you."

"Tell Maria I'll think about it."

"She says Judge Clarkson needs an answer pretty soon."

"Okay. Tell her I'll let her know tomorrow. Would you mind watching Sherman for an hour or so?"

"Sure. He's my favorite client, aren't you, Sherman?" Sherman's ears rise, twitch, and go back to their customary curl. It's his way of smiling.

A normal woman would do something nice for herself on her birthday, go to a movie or an art gallery, maybe treat herself to lunch at an expensive restaurant, but I go to the hospital to visit an old man.

I buy a *New Yorker* in the gift shop, hoping he's feeling well enough to do some reading, but when I walk into his room the man in the bed isn't Mr. Hart. I can hardly bring myself to ask about him at the nurses' station. I can't help noticing the shadow of his name, RUSSELL HART, still visible where the magic marker has been erased on the board behind the nurses. And then: "He's been transferred to Cardiology, Room 310." I share the elevator going up with a nurse pushing a man on a stretcher. The patient lies on his back, eyes closed, mouth open, so motionless I wonder if he's dead. But wouldn't they cover him with a sheet? I feel queasy.

I used to be tough. I've sat in the prosecutor's office reviewing the most gruesome photographs from the medical examiner: heads blasted by shotguns, charred skin, decomposing bodies. I've cross-examined the forensic dental expert who used bite marks on the deceased's neck to identify my client as the perpetrator. I've represented the woman whose boyfriend smashed her nose with a hammer. But here, in the hospital elevator, I'm about to faint. It's not the poor man on the stretcher; it's being in this place where life is so erasable, where death is always just around the corner.

When the elevator door opens I find a window, press my cheek against the cool glass, breathe. What am I doing here? I see myself on the witness stand being grilled by Henry Swinton, Mrs. Hart by his side.

How many times did you visit Mr. Hart in the hospital, Ms. Baynard?

Twice.

And how did that come about?

His lawyer conveyed his request that I come to the hospital.

He asked to see you on two different occasions?

He asked to see me the first time. The second time I was just . . .

You were just what, Ms. Baynard?

Visiting of my own accord.

So that would have been a social visit, right?

I was worried about him. He was very ill.

So it would be fair to say, wouldn't it, Ms. Baynard, that by the time of that second visit you'd formed some emotional bond with Mr. Hart?

I was concerned about him, that's all. He was alone.

Then Swinton delivers the blow: *And you must admit, Ms. Baynard, that your emotional bond with Mr. Hart has influenced the report you've made to the court today—that he be awarded custody of Sherman?*

But Henry Swinton won't have to grill me like this. Even if Rusty Hart survives, I know I won't recommend that he get Sherman. Sure,

Mrs. Hart is overprotective, maybe even a control freak, but she's always been the one who kept track of Sherman's appointments with Dr. Borden, made sure he had his shots, bought the right kind of dog food. As crazy as it was for her to go out in the middle of the night to rescue an abused dog, she's shown me that she really cares about animals. And now there's the issue of Mr. Hart's health.

Still, I can't imagine that day in court when I'll have to watch his face as I say, *Your honor, there's no doubt that both parties are equally committed to Sherman's welfare, but a joint custody arrange-ment is not in his best interest. Sherman needs stability. He needs to know where home is, especially as he grows older.*

It won't help much that I'll add, as a kind of consolation prize, *I propose, however, that Mr. Hart be given visitation with Sherman one afternoon a week, on a day to be agreed upon between the parties, and every other weekend.* Joe Baynard will be the one to sign the order, but Rusty Hart will always blame me for the loss of his best buddy.

If he survives his heart attack, this might kill him.

As I approach Room 310, I can hear the argument going on inside:

If you won't eat, you'll never get well.

That stuff isn't food. Take it away!

Open your mouth, Rusty!

I'm not a baby.

You're acting like one.

You could bring me something decent to eat.

What would you like?

I stop outside the half-open door, listening.

A slice of pizza.

I'm not bringing pizza to a man who's just had a nearly fatal heart attack!

You asked me what I wanted.

Eating unhealthy food is what got you into this.

What got me into this was a call from the magistrate, saying my wife was in jail.

Don't start that again.

What a damn fool thing to do!

You're going to give yourself another heart attack if you don't settle down.

Are you even grateful that I came to get you?

I'm dropping the divorce case, aren't I? You're going to need someone to take care of you.

Maryann? (His voice softens now.)

What?

Did you miss me?

I don't need to go inside.

As I walk back toward the elevator a woman is coming in my direction, holding a little girl by the hand. Her face seems vaguely familiar, maybe an old client? I lower my head, move faster—I just want to get out of the hospital—but the little girl looks straight at me. "We got lost," she says. She's four or five.

"We're not lost, honey," says the woman. "We just have to keep going down this hall . . ."

I smile and they pass, their voices trailing behind me.

"You said we're going to see my grandpa," says the girl.

"We are."

"But why does he live in the hospital?"

"He doesn't. He had something go wrong with his heart, so he's here while the doctors help him get better."

When I get back to my car I just sit for a minute, stunned, trying to imagine the scene in Room 310.

I head back to the office, down Lockwood Boulevard with the river on my right. The college sailing class is taking advantage of this bright, windy day, their sailboats darting back and forth like butterflies. I envy them: so free, so light. I wonder if it's too late for me to learn to sail. But then Gina calls. "Delores wants you to come right home."

"What's the matter?"

"It's not your mother, that's all she would say. She sounded really upset. Don't worry about Sherman, he's fine. Just go home."

Delores's eyes are swollen from crying. "It's Charlie," she says through her sobs. "He's gone."

She's already in her coat, her purse over her shoulder, ready to leave, but when I open the door she comes to me, almost falls into my arms. It feels good to have her lean on me, to hold her while she cries—this woman who's been so strong, so unshakeable until now. She manages to tell me that Charlie's sister found him in his apartment. "It was so quick," she says. "I should have been there. He died all alone."

"You couldn't have known, Delores." I don't say what I'm thinking, that maybe this is a blessing for Charlie, for her. "Would you like me to drive you home?"

"No, I'll be okay. You take care of your mama."

When she leaves I call Gina, tell her about Charlie, about Mr. Hart's visitors.

"I can't believe Anna brought the kid," she says. "I always knew you had incredible powers of persuasion."

"I didn't have anything to do with it."

"Of course you did."

"Would you mind bringing Sherman here? Just close the office, take the afternoon off."

"You okay? You sound like you've been crying yourself."

"I'm sad for Delores."

"But it's good news about the Harts."

"I guess so, but it means saying good-bye to Sherman."

"Maybe they'll give you visitation rights."

I postpone the dinner with Ellen and my other girlfriends. Ellen argues with me. "You're going to spend your birthday in that condo with your mother?"

"It'll be a threesome," I say.

"Oh, I see. The vet's coming over."

"No, not tonight."

"Don't tell me it's Joe."

"Of course not."

"Quit being so mysterious."

"It's Sherman."

"What's so special about that?" she asks.

How can I explain why I want to spend this night with a little dog who knows nothing of birthdays? If I can lure him away from my mother maybe he'll sleep at the end of my bed, and maybe when I wake in the darkness I'll feel his warmth, the twitch of his feet as he travels— who knows where?—in his dreams.

A Work in Progress

E *very case is a story,* my old law school
professor used to say.

When I left the hospital, I thought *Hart v. Hart*
had reached its final chapter. Joe Baynard signed
the order of dismissal this month. The case is
legally over, and the Harts are living together
again, but to say they're "reconciled" is a stretch.
She calls me to gripe about him; he grabs the
phone to tell me his side of the story.

"Maryann's finally gotten it through her head
that we can't afford two houses anymore," he
says. "I thought she'd agreed to sell the one
downtown, but now she's changed her mind, says
she won't live out here at the beach unless I
promise I won't ever see the girl again. I'm not
promising any such thing."

I change the subject. "How's Sherman?"

"My buddy's fine."

"How's it going with your daughter?" I'm
almost afraid to ask.

"At least we're talking. Maryann's planning a
trip to New York. I'll go with her, provided I don't
croak first."

"That sounds good."

"I just wish she had a husband—Anna, I

mean. This isn't the way it's supposed to be, a kid growing up without a father in the house."

In the background I hear Maryann Hart: "Stop harping about that!"

"Like I say, we're talking. You deserve the credit for that."

"I didn't do anything."

"It wouldn't have happened without you. Hold on, my wife wants to ask you something."

"I hope I'm not being presumptuous," Mrs. Hart says, "but when we go to New York, I want to stay long enough to have a nice visit—a week at least. Rusty's reluctant to leave Sherman at the kennel. Dr. Borden suggested you might be willing to dog-sit. Again, I don't want to seem presumptuous, and I wouldn't ask if Dr. Borden hadn't recommended you."

"I'd be happy to. I've missed him."

"We haven't made any definite plans yet. I wanted to talk to you first."

"Why don't you bring him by the office sometime? Or maybe I could drive out to the beach with my mother. She misses him, too."

My mother is still with me. When Compassionate Care called to say they had an opening in the Alzheimer's wing, I turned it down. Delores says she wants to keep working. "I'm not going to sit around and mope all day long," she says. I've hired two other sitters, one for the night shift and the other for weekends. Even with all this help I don't know how long we'll be able to manage. Last week Mom insisted she was "going away on vacation." I humored her, didn't interfere when she pulled a suitcase from the closet and started packing. It wasn't until she tried to add a bunch of ripe bananas and a jar of mayonnaise to the pile of clothes that I had to stop her.

Sometimes I think, *this isn't my mother.* My real mother is still a presence in my life. She's still following me around the kitchen, so close I feel her breath on my back. "You might add a little salt to that soup," my real mother says. Or when we're sitting on the balcony watching the ships come and go in the harbor, she's giving me advice about my love life, about how I should be careful not to ruin things this time, because "Darling, this could be your last chance."

My real mother and I still argue all the time. It grieves her that I'm not sure I believe in life after death—at least not in her kind of heaven. She fears for my soul, she says. She wants us to be together in heaven someday. "If you don't believe," she says, "you'll risk eternal damnation." *Don't worry,* I reply, *if you nag God enough, I'm sure he'll make some allowance.*

Every now and then, in these imaginary conversations, one of us says something unexpected. She apologizes for giving Brownie away. "It broke your heart," she says, "to lose your father, and then to lose that dog, too." I tell her I'm sorry I never gave her enough credit for being so brave after Dad died, going back to work, persevering. I tell her I know she did the best she could. My real mother can't quite bring herself to apologize for the way she behaved after I left Joe, blaming me for everything. But I don't expect miracles.

Shortly after he signed the order of dismissal in *Hart v. Hart*, the Honorable Joseph H. Baynard moved back home. Last week I saw him coming toward me on Broad Street and I expected him to nod, smile, and keep going, as he's done the last couple of times we've seen each other, but he stopped. "How are things?" he asked.

"Fine," I answered. "You?"

"Better."

"I was glad to hear about you and Susan."

"It's still a work in progress," he said.

"Isn't it always?"

"You must have thought I'd lost my mind," he said.

"You were going through a bad time."

"But you were still mad as hell at me, and I deserved it. How's your mother?" I gave him a brief report. "Tell her I'm thinking about her," he said before we shook hands. The handshake lasted longer than it should, a second or two beyond mere friendship, and after we parted I realize *I* was the one holding on, not Joe.

· · ·

I spent last weekend with Tony Borden at his house not far from the clinic. It was chilly, but one night we snuggled in the hammock on his screened porch, under a blanket, watching the sun go down behind the marshes.

"It's so peaceful out there," I said. "Hard to believe we're only twenty miles from the city." I was already feeling guilty about leaving my mother, though she'd seemed fine when I'd left her with the new weekend sitter.

"It's an illusion," Tony said. "Nature isn't all that peaceful. Right now the snakes are coming out to hunt, the owls are scouring the field for mice, and the vultures have just about finished off that dead deer you saw on the way out."

"I never thought of it that way."

"The only difference is, the animals are just doing it to survive. So in my opinion, they're nobler than humans. Except for you, of course. I make an exception for you." He reached down to rub the beagle's forehead. "You sure you won't take her?"

"Maybe after I get Mom settled in with her new sitters. Right now I just don't see how I can handle a dog full-time."

"You did okay with Sherman."

"I'll think about it."

"That seems to be your standard line."

He's been moody lately. His son is coming for

a visit over Christmas. Tony's worried about how it will go. I try to be reassuring, though I have my own worries. Will Jake like me? I've represented hundreds of children over the years, but what do I really know about twelve-year-old boys?

And last weekend Tony said *I love you.*

I wasn't ready for that.

"What are you waiting for?" asks Gina when I tell her about my hesitation.

If my mother could speak she'd undoubtedly say, *Don't mess it up. This might be your last chance.*

"He's perfect for you," says my friend Ellen.

Sherman seems to have an opinion, too. I keep a picture of him on my desk, the photo that was once part of the court file. When I'm overwhelmed with work, like today, his dark eyes look right at me, bright and wise, steady: *I'm glad you took that cat case. Even a cat deserves a good lawyer.*

Center Point Large Print
600 Brooks Road / PO Box 1
Thorndike, ME 04986-0001 USA

(207) 568-3717

US & Canada:
1 800 929-9108
www.centerpointlargeprint.com